THE BOOKS OF
ELSEWHERE
volume four

THE STRANGERS

THE BOOKS OF
ELSEWHERE

volume four

THE STRANGERS

by Jacqueline West

illustrated by Poly Bernatene

DIAL BOOKS FOR YOUNG READERS
an imprint of Penguin Group (USA) Inc.

DIAL BOOKS FOR YOUNG READERS
A division of Penguin Young Readers Group
Published by the Penguin Group
Penguin Group (USA) Inc., 375 Hudson Street, New York, NY 10014, U.S.A.

USA/Canada/UK/Ireland/Australia/New Zealand/India/South Africa/China
Penguin Books Ltd, Registered Offices: 80 Strand, London WC2R 0RL, England
For more information about the Penguin Group visit penguin.com

Library of Congress Cataloging-in-Publication Data
West, Jacqueline, date.
The strangers / by Jacqueline West ; illustrated by Poly Bernatene.
p. cm. — (The books of Elsewhere ; v. 4)
Summary: "When something crucial goes missing, twelve-year-old Olive and her friends must
decide how to get it back—put their faith in a strange and dangerous magic, their odd new
neighbors, or someone more uncertain and terrifying than both" —Provided by publisher.
ISBN 978-0-8037-3690-0 (hardcover)
[1. Space and time—Fiction. 2. Dwellings—Fiction. 3. Magic—Fiction.
4. Lost and found possessions—Fiction.] I. Bernatene, Poly, ill. II. Title.
PZ7.W51776Str 2013
[Fic]—dc23
2012040004

Printed in the U.S.A.

1 3 5 7 9 10 8 6 4 2

Designed by Jennifer Kelly
Text set in Requiem

ALWAYS LEARNING   PEARSON

For Sherri and Glenn—
fearless adventurers
—JW

THE BOOKS OF
ELSEWHERE
volume four

THE STRANGERS

HOUSES ARE GOOD at keeping secrets.
They shut out light. They muffle sounds.

Some have musty attics and murky basements. Some have closets stacked with sealed boxes and locked rooms where no one ever goes. A house can stand with its windows curtained and its doors shut for decades—even centuries—without revealing a hint of what is hidden inside.

The old stone house on Linden Street had kept its secrets for a very long time. For more than a hundred years, it had loomed at the crest of the hill, its towering black rooftops piercing a canopy of ancient trees. A pool of shadows surrounded the house, even on the sunniest days. Overgrown hedges enclosed its garden. Its deep-set windows were blurry and dark. Even in the height of summer, its stone walls exhaled a faint, grave-like chill, as though warmth and sunlight could never quite get in, and the darkness inside could never quite get out.

But as this particular summer dwindled into autumn, and the ancient trees dropped their leaves, and the nights grew long and cool and dark, the secrets hidden in the old stone house seemed to rise, at long last, to the surface.

On those lingering autumn evenings, dim red and purple lights began to glow from the house's upper windows, where the silhouettes of watchful cats sat motionless on the sills. Cobwebs stretched across the porch. Headstones sprouted from the overgrown lawn, jutting up like crooked gray teeth. After sunset, when darkness covered the house, small, fiery faces flickered from the shadows around the front door.

Neighbors walking down Linden Street had always walked a bit faster as they passed the old stone house. Now they ran.

As for the people living inside those chilly stone walls: They were delighted to know that their house looked so frightening.

It *was* almost Halloween, after all.

Inside the old stone house were the three Dunwoodys: Alec Dunwoody, a mathematician; Alice Dunwoody, another mathematician; and their daughter, Olive Dunwoody, who was about as likely to become a mathematician as she was to become a three-toed tree sloth.

Throughout the twelve years of Olive's life, the Dunwoodys had lived in many different towns, moving from apartment to apartment as Mr. and Mrs. Dunwoody moved from one mathematical job to another. When they had settled on Linden Street early that summer, Mr. and Mrs. Dunwoody were happy to think that at last they had a real house all to themselves.

But the truth was: They didn't.

A trio of cats—Horatio, Leopold, and Harvey—had been keeping watch over the old stone house since long before the Dunwoodys arrived. Also hidden in its quiet rooms were a slew of sleepy neighbors, three stonemasons, a bouncy brown dog, several dancing girls in gauzy dresses, a café packed with Parisians, an out-of-practice orchestra, a castle porter, a woman in a bathtub, whole forests of trees, entire flocks of birds, and one small boy in a white nightshirt.

Mr. and Mrs. Dunwoody had no idea that they had so many roommates. But Olive knew. Thanks to a pair of spectacles she'd discovered in an upstairs drawer, Olive had learned the truth about the paintings that gleamed from the house's cold stone walls.

Olive knew that Aldous McMartin, the house's original owner, had been a very talented—very unusual—artist. Each painting he created was a living, changeless world, full of flowers that never wilted, and moons that never set, and people that could never die.

People like Aldous's beloved granddaughter, Annabelle.

People like Aldous McMartin himself.

These painted worlds also made the perfect hiding place for everything Aldous wanted to conceal. Family spellbooks. Nosy neighbors. Dangerously curious almost-twelve-year-old girls who moved into your house and started unearthing all of its secrets.

Inside Aldous's paintings, Olive had been chased by shadows, nearly drowned, and almost buried alive. She had survived each threat so far, but Olive didn't know how much longer her good luck would hold. She'd already set the living image of Annabelle free, and worse still, she'd let Aldous's final self-portrait slip through her fingers straight into his granddaughter's cold, painted hands. As soon as Annabelle found a way to release him from the canvas, Olive's luck would take a turn for the much, much worse.

Back in their college days, Mr. and Mrs. Dunwoody had invented a card game called 42—a more complicated version of 21—where each player tries to collect 42 points without going over. Sometimes, when

Olive was really bored, her parents convinced her to play it with them, even though she never won. In her struggle with the McMartins, Olive felt as if she'd flipped one low card after another. Even if she didn't exactly understand the mathematical rules of probability, Olive knew that a lucky streak couldn't go on forever. Each good card brought a bad card closer. At any moment, the face of a chilly, smiling queen, or a stony, sunken-eyed king would stare up at her, and she would lose, yet again.

Compared to this very real fear, Halloween began to seem downright cheery.

So Olive had hung the cobwebs and put up the colored lights. She had cut out the cat silhouettes, modeling them on the house's real (and much more talkative) cats. She had carved the jack-o'-lanterns with her parents, sitting on the porch in the October twilight. Mr. Dunwoody's jack-o'-lantern was made up entirely of equilateral triangles. Mrs. Dunwoody's jack-o'-lantern was made up of three scalene triangles and one complex quadrilateral. Olive's jack-o'-lantern was made up of a jagged nose, two asymmetrical squinting eyes, and a crooked, snarling mouth, which disturbed her parents and the neighbors for entirely different reasons.

When she was finished decorating, Olive had stood at the curb looking up at her towering, terrifying house, and she'd felt a momentary zing of pride. For once, *she* might be the one getting to frighten someone else.

But being frightened wasn't Olive's real problem. Olive's real problem was the feeling that—even with the cats and a few human friends, and all the painted people surrounding her—down at the very bottom, where the house's worst secrets lived, she was completely alone.

Olive was the one who had unearthed the house's secrets. She was the one who would bear the brunt of the McMartins' anger, if—or *when*—they did come back. Sometimes Olive felt as though she were carrying the weight of the entire house, with its massive stone walls and its huge, dim rooms, inside of her worn purple backpack. It would have been nice to let someone else carry it for a while.

Weeks ago, after Annabelle had made off with Aldous's portrait, Horatio had promised Olive that they might not have to face the McMartins all by themselves. Since then, however, he'd gotten suspiciously secretive about the matter.

"But what did you *mean?*" Olive demanded for what might have been the hundredth time, when she and the huge orange cat were alone together in the backyard. Olive had been raking leaves and throwing herself into the piles. The leaves crunched around her as she sat up and looked at Horatio, who was seated near the shriveled lilac hedge, his eyes fixed on the empty gray house just beyond. "You said, 'We may not have to fight alone.'"

"Did I?" said Horatio.

"Yes." Olive tugged a maple leaf out of her hair. "You did."

"Then I must have meant what I said," replied the cat.

Olive flopped back into the pile. "You're keeping something from me."

"If I am," Horatio's voice murmured through the crackling of the leaves, "you should trust that I am doing so for good reasons."

Olive tried to believe this. But as the autumn days blew by, and no new help appeared, and Horatio went on refusing to explain, Olive felt more alone than ever.

She was the only student in her art class who couldn't touch a paintbrush without shivering. She was the only one on the school bus who spent the whole ride peering anxiously out of the windows, sure that she would catch sight of a pair of painted eyes staring back in. She was the only kid in sixth grade who wasn't excitedly making plans for a Halloween costume, because she knew she wouldn't be safe outdoors, at night, in the danger-cloaking darkness, without the walls of the old stone house standing solidly all around her.

If anyone had told her that something was about to happen that would make Olive's current aloneness feel as friendly as a birthday party, she simply wouldn't have believed it.

So it was probably just as well that no one did.

A FTER THE LAST bell had rung on the final school day of October, Olive made a beeline for the bus. The sooner she got out of this twisting brick building, the sooner she would be on her way back to the old stone house. There were cats to confer with, and rooms to check, and painted people to visit, and she didn't want to waste one extra minute entangled in the halls of the junior high. Olive careened around a corner and smashed straight into a girl headed in the opposite direction, bumping her so hard with her heavy backpack that the girl spun in a circle. The girl's armload of bright orange papers fluttered through the air, like strangely rectangular autumn leaves.

"Hey!" the girl shouted. "Watch where you're going!"

"Oh," Olive mumbled, stumbling backward. "I'm sorry."

With a huff, the girl bent down to gather the papers. Olive crouched beside her. Even through her lowered eyelashes, she could see that the girl's hair was sleek and dark, and her green-brown eyes were framed by eyeliner. Olive looked back at the floor.

"I hope I didn't wreck anything," she said, straightening up with the papers in one outstretched hand.

"That's okay," the girl sighed. "I've got about a billion more to give out anyway." She crammed the pages back into the stack. "Are you coming?"

Olive blinked. "Coming where?"

"To the *carnival?*" The girl shook the stack of papers, making their edges fan and rustle. "To the Halloween carnival that's happening *tomorrow,* that's all over the flyers you were just holding in your hands?"

"Oh." Olive's mind took off like a mouse in a maze, bumping its whiskery nose at each turn. *Is this a test? If I say yes, will this girl roll her eyes and say "Oh, great"? If I say no, will she laugh and say "Good"? If I say I don't know, will she say—*

"If you say 'I don't know,' I'll scream," said the girl, widening her outlined eyes. "That's what *everybody's* been saying. We did all this work getting everything ready, and I've gotten about a million paper cuts from these stupid flyers, and somebody had *better* show up."

"Oh," said Olive again. "I—I don't know."

The girl didn't scream. She just sighed again and ran her hand through her long, sleek hair. Olive caught a glimpse of orange fingernails with tiny black pumpkins perfectly placed on each tip. "Is there some other, cooler party happening that I just haven't heard about?" the girl asked.

If there was another, cooler party, Olive hadn't heard about it either. "I don't think so," she said.

"Are you going trick-or-treating instead of coming to the carnival?" the girl demanded. "Because you can do both, you know."

"Probably not."

The girl frowned. "Why not?"

Because two witches made of paint will do terrible things to me if they get the chance. Olive swallowed. "Um . . ."

"You should come. It'll be fun. Here." The girl shoved a flyer into Olive's hands. "Bring your friends." With a swish of glossy hair, she strode off around the corner.

Olive looked down at the paper in her hands.

HALLOWEEN CARNIVAL!
Costume Contest!! Haunted Mazes!!
Caramel Apples!! Fabulous Prizes!!!

Too many exclamation points!!! thought Olive. But she folded the flyer and tucked it into her pocket anyway.

She was still thinking about the carnival when she and Rutherford Dewey climbed off the school bus at the foot of Linden Street.

"You don't mind staying home on Halloween, do you?" Olive asked as they crunched their way up the leafy sidewalk.

"I understand your hesitation," said Rutherford, in his rapid, slightly nasal voice. "You are probably right that leaving the house at night would make you vulnerable. My grandmother's charms are surrounding the place, so as long as you stay inside, they should keep you safe as well."

"But—" Olive began.

"But then again, the McMartins have found a way around those protections before."

Olive glanced at Rutherford out of the corner of her eye. Having a friend who could read her thoughts came in handy sometimes. Other times, it was simply irritating. "That's just what I was going to say," she said, under her breath.

They had reached the walkway to Mrs. Dewey's house, which nestled a short distance away from the street, behind a knot of shady birch trees. Mrs. Dewey herself was bent over in front of the house, tending to a cluster of plants. Her wide, round backside glided back and forth above her tiny feet, like a blimp anchored to a pair of high heels. She looked up as Rutherford and Olive approached.

"Hello, you two!" she called in her flute-like voice. She bent down again, making the blimp waver, before straightening up with a small paper package in one hand. "Olive, as I heard you weren't going trick-or-treating this year, I made you a sample to bring home. They're my chocolate gingerbread bars and frosted pumpkin-spice drops," she said, pressing the bag into Olive's hands.

"Thank you, Mrs. Dewey," said Olive.

"In return, you can help me gather some leaves." Mrs. Dewey gestured to the shrubs beside her. "This Matchstick Mallow is about to go dormant for the winter."

"What are you using Matchstick Mallow for, Grandma?" asked Rutherford, beginning to tug the pale leaves from their twigs.

"I like to keep a small stock on hand." Mrs. Dewey lowered her voice slightly, in case any neighbors were near enough to hear. "It's good for easing fears, in infusions and so forth—as long as you don't use too much. A little fear is a good thing. It can protect you, like a shield."

Rutherford's eyes lit up. "A knight's shield?" he asked. "What type would it be? Pavise? Buckler? Targe?"

"I'm sure I don't know, Rutherford," said Mrs. Dewey wearily.

Olive snapped a leaf off of its stem. It had a petaled shape, almost like a five-leafed clover, and it felt spongy and smooth against her skin.

"Wouldn't Martyr's Hope be a more effective ingredient for eliminating fear?" Rutherford asked.

Mrs. Dewey's soft, round body turned suddenly stiff. She swiveled toward Rutherford. "Where did you hear of Martyr's Hope?"

"In the book I've been reading, the one about the medieval magician's herbarium. It was on your bookshelf."

Mrs. Dewey sighed. She tugged another leaf off of the shrub, placing it in the jar at her feet, before answering. "Martyr's Hope is a volatile, unpredictable plant. I don't raise it, and I wouldn't use it if I did."

Rutherford straightened his smudgy wire-rimmed glasses, looking puzzled. "But isn't it one of the ingredients used in creating Calling Candles?"

"*Calling Candles?* RUTHERFORD DEWEY." Mrs. Dewey's voice changed from a flute into a trombone. "I don't use such items, and I expect you to be wise enough never to use them either," she added more quietly. "Making such a thing—and using it—takes dark and dangerous magic."

"I see," said Rutherford calmly. He plucked another leaf. "And what do Calling Candles look like?"

Mrs. Dewey let out a sigh that could have inflated a hot-air balloon.

"If I can't identify a Calling Candle, isn't it possible that I could use one by accident?" Rutherford asked, before Mrs. Dewey could speak. "Like sitting down for a picnic in a patch of Poison Oak?"

"Rutherford . . ." Mrs. Dewey pressed one hand to her forehead. "Calling Candles are bluish, and have a powdery silver surface, a bit like frost on a window-pane. They can also be used only *once,* and it's awfully unlikely that you would happen to find one, light it, and say someone's name into the flames by *accident.*" Mrs. Dewey halted. She pressed her lips together and stared down at her grandson. "I've told you more than enough. And don't you even *try* to read it out of me. You know I can keep you out." She examined the glass jar. "I believe that's enough Mallow to last for the winter—unless either of you is expecting to have an especially frightening one." Mrs. Dewey gave a little start and turned toward Olive, looking as though she'd like to take those words back. "And I'm sure there's no reason you *would,*" she added.

Olive nodded at Mrs. Dewey. But she wasn't nearly so sure.

After waving good-bye to Rutherford and his grandmother, Olive headed up the street, hurrying past the deserted gray hulk of the Nivens house before cutting across her own front yard. She ducked under the canopy of cobwebs and clomped onto the porch. Dead ferns whispered from their hanging baskets. The porch swing creaked softly in the breeze. Olive tested the doorknob, making sure it was still locked, before fitting the key into its slot.

The door opened inward with a groan.

Olive sniffed the now-familiar scents of dust and wax and old wood, and listened to the silence that washed in to erase the sound of the opening door. Along the hall, dust motes glimmered in a beam of faint sunlight, beckoning her onward. For a moment, Olive felt sure that the house wasn't just watching her, but *recognizing* her. With a last deep breath of crisp autumn air, she stepped over the threshold.

"Hello, Olive," said a voice from the parlor doorway. Horatio's wide orange face peered out into the hall.

"Hello, Horatio," Olive answered, locking the door behind her again. "Anything strange happen today?"

"Not a thing. Unless you call Harvey chaining himself to the upstairs banister 'strange,' and I no longer do."

Olive dropped her backpack to the hardwood floor. "Was he being Hairy Houdini again?"

"He was."

"And did you rescue him?"

"I did."

"Thank you, Horatio." Olive tossed her jacket over the knobby brass coatrack and headed for the staircase. "I'm going to pay Morton a visit before my parents get home."

"An excellent idea," said Horatio, stepping back into the parlor with a swish of his plumy tail.

"Oh, by the way," Olive called over the banister, "what did you mean about us not having to fight alone?"

Horatio didn't turn around. "Nice try, Olive."

Olive let out a sigh. Then she jogged the rest of the way up the staircase.

In the upstairs hall, Olive pulled the spectacles out of her collar and settled them on her nose. The paintings along each wall rippled to life. Inside one frame, the silvery lake sent delicate waves toward the shore. In another, bare trees rattled above a moonlit path. In the painting of the Scottish hills, bracken tossed and fluttered like a golden sea.

Olive remembered the taste of that silvery lake water filling her mouth as the rising waves dragged her under. She remembered the darkness swirling behind those bare trees, rushing down to surround her like a swarm of shadowy insects. She remembered the hole waiting in that golden bracken—the hole that had nearly trapped her until her body turned to paint and she was stuck there, not living, not dying, forever.

With a shudder, Olive hurried toward the painting of Linden Street.

The canvas squished around her like a sheet of warm Jell-O. She plunged through the frame, head-first, and landed with a whump in the misty grass on the other side.

The Linden Street of a century ago wound its way up the hill before her. The houses along the street were sleepy and silent, but here and there, burning candles bobbed behind lace curtains. The wary eyes of painted neighbors peered out at Olive as she raced by.

On the sidewalk before one towering gray house, a small boy in a large white nightshirt was waiting. He straightened up as Olive drew nearer.

"Catch!" he yelled.

Olive ducked.

A rock zoomed straight toward the crown of her head. Just before it could smack her, it arced backward and rolled to a stop near the boy's bare feet.

"Morton!" Olive shouted. "That was mean!"

"I told you to catch it," said Morton.

"You know I'm not a good catcher!"

"Yes, but I also knew it would come right back again before it even hit you," said Morton. "Probably."

Olive stalked past Morton and plunked down on his front steps, still scowling.

Morton wavered on the walkway in front of her. "I

didn't think you were coming today," he said, after a moment. "I waited and waited."

"Keep throwing rocks at my head, and I won't come *at all*," said Olive.

Morton dug one toe into the ground and twisted from side to side, his tufty white hair turned translucent by the glow of a neighbor's candle. Olive watched his head droop lower and lower until she thought it might topple him straight to the ground, like a pumpkin on a skinny stem.

"I'm sorry I was late," said Olive at last. "I stopped at Mrs. Dewey's house for a little while."

Morton didn't look at her. "You've hardly been here all week."

"I'm sorry," said Olive again. "I had lots of homework. And it was my birthday last weekend, and I've been decorating the house for Halloween."

From the slump of Morton's shoulders, Olive could tell that her explanation wasn't helping. He plopped down on the grass beyond the stoop and wrapped his arms around his knobby knees. "Did you get presents?"

"Yes."

"What did you get?"

"Rutherford gave me a book about Renaissance paintings. My mom and dad gave me a new coat and some sketchbooks and a locker mirror."

"A locker mirror?"

"A little mirror to hang in my locker at school. The frame is all made out of numbers, and it says 'Here's looking at Euclid!' on the front."

Morton frowned. "I don't get it."

"Me neither."

Morton rested his chin on his folded arms. "I would have given you a birthday present," he said.

For a minute, neither of them spoke. Then Morton said, in a clearer, firmer voice, "When it's my turn with the spectacles, we should have *another* birthday party. For you *and* me. And you should have to give me presents for all the birthdays that I've missed."

Olive's heart gave a nervous leap—and it wasn't at the thought of having to buy Morton dozens of presents. She had promised him that if she didn't find his parents by the end of November, he could have the spectacles in order to search for them himself. Olive had looked everywhere for some sign of Mary and Harold Nivens. She'd searched the house, she'd explored Elsewhere, she'd even questioned her neighbors on Linden Street (one of whom had turned out to be a painting herself), but she'd found no promising clues. For a while, Olive had hoped that by re-creating Morton's parents in Aldous's magical paints she could sidestep the problem completely. But her portrait of the Nivenses had turned out all wrong—and now, with only one month to go, she was no closer to finding the *real* Nivenses, either.

"You know how dangerous it will be, don't you?" she asked, looking down into Morton's moon-like face. "Elsewhere is full of things that can hurt you or trap you. And the outside is even worse. You'll have to keep your skin covered up, so no one figures out the truth about you, and so you don't get hurt by light, or fire, or—"

"I'm *already* trapped in here," Morton interrupted. "And I'm sick of missing everything. School. And birthdays. And Halloweens." He hopped to his feet. "I miss *everything.*"

Before Olive could reply, Morton charged toward the stoop and started kicking at the porch banisters, his bare feet smacking against the sharp-edged wood. The posts began to splinter.

"Morton!" Olive jumped up. "Don't! You'll hurt yourself!"

"It doesn't matter," said Morton, stopping. The banisters straightened themselves, splinters mending, paint sealing. "Everything just goes back to the way it was." Morton looked down as a fresh red wound on his foot faded back into unbroken skin. "I don't like it."

Olive stood beside him, her hands shoved uselessly into her pockets. The folded flyer dug its corner into her palm.

"Morton," she began, "what if there was a way for you to come out of Elsewhere for a little while?"

Morton's head rose.

"Just for Halloween," Olive added. "But you would miss one less thing." She paused, chewing the inside of her lip. "Do you think you would like that?"

Morton looked up at her, narrowing his eyes. "Do *you* think I would like it?"

"Yes. I think so."

Morton gave her a knowing nod. "I thought so too."

Olive had gotten back out of the painting and down the stairs to the kitchen just in time to hear the front door bang.

"Hello, 12.02-year-old!" called Mr. Dunwoody from the entry.

"I believe it would be 12.0178, dear," said Mrs. Dunwoody.

"I'm rounding up," said Mr. Dunwoody, striding down the hall and through the kitchen door. He beamed at Olive, who was settled innocently at the table with her worn copy of *Alice in Wonderland*. "How many times would you say you've read that book?"

"I don't know," said Olive. "Maybe thirty?"

"Wrong!" sang Mr. Dunwoody. "Seventeen. I've kept track."

Olive slipped a bookmark between the pages and watched her mother set a pot of water on the stovetop. "Um . . . Mom and Dad?" she began. "Remember how

I said I wasn't going to dress up and go out on Halloween this year?"

"Yes," prompted her parents.

"Now I think I will." Olive rubbed her fingers across *Alice in Wonderland*'s worn cloth cover. "But I need to come up with a costume, fast."

"Let's see." Mr. Dunwoody adjusted his glasses. "I've got a simple one: You could cut arm and leg holes in a large box, and wear a plant on your head."

"What?" said Olive.

"You would be a *square root*. Get it?"

"No," said Olive.

"How about Hypatia?" Mrs. Dunwoody suggested, taking a box of pasta from the cabinet. "All you would need is a toga."

"Who?" said Olive.

"Hypatia," Mrs. Dunwoody repeated. "The first famous woman in mathematics? The last librarian of the library of Alexandria?"

"I don't know," said Olive. "That doesn't sound very Halloween-y."

"You don't think so?" Mrs. Dunwoody's eyebrows went up. "She was accused of being a witch and killed by an angry mob."

"Oh," said Olive as the word *witch* sent a gush of ice water through her stomach. "Maybe."

Mrs. Dunwoody turned back to the stove. "Ninety-two . . ." she counted to herself, shaking a stream of pasta shells into the pot. "One hundred and ten. There we are."

Mr. Dunwoody, who had been watching the noodles plop into the water, bolted suddenly upright. "Eureka!" he exclaimed. "You could be Archimedes, leaping out of the bath after discovering his principle of displacement! You wouldn't need a costume at all!" Mr. Dunwoody tapped his chin thoughtfully. "Of course, it might be wiser—if more inaccurate—to wear a towel."

"That might be a little *too* scary," said Olive.

"I think it's a wonderful suggestion, darling," said Mrs. Dunwoody, patting her husband's shoulder. "Perhaps you should use it yourself."

Olive pictured her father opening the door to a cluster of trick-or-treaters while wearing this particular Halloween costume. If the house itself didn't scare them away, Mr. Dunwoody in nothing but a bath towel probably would.

"Thank you," she said, before her parents could supply any more ideas. "I'll think of something."

Olive hoped she was right. She had to think of something, for Morton's sake. And she had to think fast.

T HE NEXT MORNING, Olive tore up the stairs with two strawberry waffles still bouncing in her stomach. If she was going to leave the house after dark, she was going to bring protection along—which meant she had a lot of work to do in very little time.

She raced down the hall into the pink bedroom. The sky outside was too gray and dim to send the usual scattering of sunny spots through the curtains, but the air held its familiar scent of mothballs and dust, along with a whiff of dried flower petals so faint that it was almost an illusion.

Olive placed the spectacles on her nose and headed for the room's single large painting: an ancient town somewhere in Italy or Greece, with a huge stone archway guarded by two towering stone soldiers. Olive dove toward the painted arch, feeling the surface of the canvas wriggle around her as she plunged into the tiny entryway beyond.

There was no light here; nothing but the faintly glowing band that outlined the edges of a door. Olive lunged through the darkness, grasping the doorknob. The door swung open before her with a low, heavy groan, like a very large creature turning over in its sleep.

A narrow flight of wooden stairs angled upward from the doorway. Olive climbed them gingerly, avoiding the papery corpses of wasps and dehydrated flies that clustered in the corners. At the top of the staircase, Olive paused, blinking around at the cluttered attic. A few streaks of dusty daylight fell through the round windows, scattering shadows everywhere. Antique furniture draped in ghostly white sheets loomed against the walls. Stacks of old steamer trunks towered toward the rafters. Silent clocks, unframed canvases, dead telephones, and one small, battered cannon glinted at Olive from the corners. If there was anywhere in the old stone house to find an interesting Halloween costume, it was here.

Olive crept toward the center of the room, where Aldous McMartin's easel stood in its patch of pale sun. Olive had brought the easel back to its place after Annabelle had fled with Aldous's last painting, and now she noticed that the attic's other furnishings seemed almost to lean away from it, as if it were some strange, potentially dangerous animal. Its shelf was bare now, its drop cloth gone—and still the sight of the easel, patiently waiting, made the back of Olive's neck start to prickle. The prickle grew into a chill that stiffened the strands of her hair.

Olive knew what this meant. *She was being watched.*

She whirled around to find herself staring down the length of a cardboard tube, straight into one glittering green eye.

"Ahoy there, matey," growled the cat at the other end of the tube. "I spotted ye through my spyglass. Not much escapes the single eye of wily Captain Black-paw!" The cat leaped away from the hat rack where his "spyglass" was braced, and Olive caught a glimpse of a tiny leather eyepatch and a splotchily colored tail before he bounded off into the rafters.

"Ahoy, Captain," Olive called toward the ceiling. "How are things on board ship?"

"Smooth sailing," snarled Harvey's voice from above. "Ye know the old adage: 'Red sky at night: A sailor's stoplight. Green sky at dawn: Sailor, sail on!'"

"Green sky?" Olive repeated.

Harvey executed a tumbling leap from one rafter to another. "Prepare to set sail for the islands!" he commanded his imaginary crew. "All paws on deck!"

"Um . . . Harvey? Or Captain Blackpaw?" Olive

began, watching the cat dive-bomb a dusty armchair and spring back toward the beams. "I came to ask you something."

"Ask away! Ha-HA!" roared Harvey, scampering across the shoulders of an old sewing dummy.

"Today is Halloween. And I'm going to take Morton out, in disguise, so he doesn't have to miss it." Harvey paused, aiming his one un-patched eye in Olive's direction. "Rutherford is coming along. Leopold and Horatio said they would escort us, so I have to make their costumes too," Olive went on. "And I wondered—will you come with us? In a costume, I mean?"

Harvey lost his footing on the sewing dummy. He hit the attic floor with a thump. A moment later, his face reappeared, inching out from beneath a velvet love seat.

"*Will* I?" he whispered.

"That's what I just asked you."

Harvey's eyes were glazed. "That's what you just asked me."

Olive watched Harvey's gaze drift worshipfully toward the rafters, as if all the heroes of history and literature were gathered there in invisible feline form.

"I'll take that as a yes," said Olive. "I'm in a big hurry already, so I hope you won't mind making your own costume. Will you?"

"*Will* I?" Harvey echoed, still staring at the ceiling.

"Good," said Olive.

While Harvey disappeared back into the clutter, Olive rushed toward the nearest corner and tore into a stack of boxes. The first three were filled with a set of fancy china. In the fourth, she found a cache of spidery lace doilies, and in the fifth, she uncovered a stack of old tablecloths, some thick and silky, some as delicate as tissue paper. An idea began to flicker in Olive's mind.

As she hauled the tablecloths out of the box, she couldn't help but picture them draped across the dining table two floors below, with the McMartin family gathered all around. McMartin hands had brushed this lacy tablecloth. These linen napkins had lain in McMartin laps. As though they were used tissues instead of fancy fabrics, Olive dumped the cloths into a heap on the floor. They wouldn't remind her of the McMartins when she was done with them.

In one small metal trunk, she uncovered a pair of old driving goggles—the kind people wore when twenty-five miles per hour seemed astonishingly fast—and a pair of leather driving gloves. Olive wriggled her hands into the gloves. She placed the goggles on top of her head. Then she hurried across the floor to look into one of the mirrors, still arranged in the circle where she had left them months ago. Looking back at her from the dusty reflection was a gangly girl in spectacles, with what looked like a pair of bulbous eyes poking out of the top of her head, and two big, brown, claw-like hands.

"Rraaahhhrrr," she growled at the mirror. And, all at once, Olive knew just what she was going to be for Halloween.

With an armload of tablecloths, several wire hangers, some curtain fringe, the goggles and gloves, and an old silk sash, Olive ran back down the attic stairs through the painting and along the hall to her own bedroom. There, she hunkered down for several hours of secret and serious work.

At precisely 4:00 that afternoon, there was a knock at the front door of the old stone house.

Olive skidded along the slippery wood of the downstairs hall. She stood on her toes to peer through the window. Two brown eyes, blurred by a pair of smudgy glasses, stared back at her.

Olive gave her wire-hanger wings a last tweak. She pulled down the driving goggles, which she had painted with wisps of flame. Then she yanked open the door.

"Grrraaaawwwwlllaallllwww!" she roared.

Rutherford blinked calmly back at her. "Good afternoon."

Olive pushed the goggles onto her forehead. Rutherford was dressed in spotless beige slacks and a tweed jacket, with a bow tie knotted snugly under his chin. It was a change from his usual uniform of wrinkly dragon T-shirts, but it certainly didn't make Olive think of Halloween.

"Why aren't you in a costume?" she asked.

"I *am*," said Rutherford. "I'm a medieval historian who teaches at a university, obviously. I'm wearing a *blazer*."

"Oh," said Olive.

"And what are you?" Rutherford asked as Olive stepped aside to let him into the hall.

"I'm a jabberwocky. See?" Olive held up her hands in the old leather gloves, with wooden tent pegs poking through the knuckles. "The claws. The wings." She pointed one tent peg at her goggles. "The eyes of flame."

"And the brown sweat suit with painted squiggles?"

"They're supposed to look like scales," said Olive, shutting the front door. A draft of cool air, spiced by the scent of burning leaves, wafted along the hallway.

"And what is *he* supposed to be?" asked Rutherford as a furry green blob tried to slink inconspicuously up the staircase.

Olive grabbed Horatio before he could skulk out of sight. "He said he didn't care what he was, so to go with my costume, I made him a mome rath." She adjusted the plastic pig snout tied around the cat's face. "Isn't he perfect?"

Above the snout, Horatio gave Olive a look that said he would like to see a long, slow bout of food poisoning inflicted on anyone who had ever dressed up her cats for Halloween.

"And wait until you see the others," Olive whispered, leading Rutherford across the entryway. "I made Leopold's costume just the way he requested it. Harvey's making something for himself. But the *surprise* turned out best of all." She glanced along the hallway toward the kitchen, where Mr. and Mrs. Dunwoody were cheerfully dividing their total number of candies among the estimated total of trick-or-treaters. "Let's get them while my parents are still busy. Come on."

Followed by a reluctant Horatio, Olive and Rutherford hustled up to the pink bedroom.

Olive put on the spectacles and Rutherford held Horatio's green tail as they climbed through the picture frame and entered the attic.

A cat the size and color of a miniature panther stood waiting for them at the top of the narrow wooden staircase.

"Good evening, miss," said the cat, with a dignified bow. "Good evening, sir."

"Good evening, Leopold," said Rutherford. "From the medals and sash, I would guess that you are portraying a high-ranking military officer, but I am not certain which one."

Leopold puffed out his glossy black chest. "The Duke of Wellington," he replied, in his deepest voice. "At your service."

"Ah! Fascinating, although the Napoleonic Wars are beyond my areas of expertise," said Rutherford, beginning to jiggle excitedly from foot to foot. "My knowledge of anything beyond the sixteenth century is fairly spotty, although I'm an expert on the Middle Ages in Western Europe—Britain and France in particular."

"Where is Harvey?" Olive asked, before Rutherford could go on. "Is he ready?"

"I'm sure he's planning his grand entrance," said Horatio.

On cue, a lumpy shape in a hooded robe shuffled out onto the rafters. It paused beneath a cluster of empty cans that dangled like church bells from the ceiling. With a jump, it grasped the rope that dangled between the cans, setting off a cacophonous clanking that grew louder and louder as it swung back and forth.

"Sanctuary!" the lump howled. "Sanctuary!"

"What is *that*?" Olive asked.

Horatio let out a sigh. "The Hunchcat of Notre Dame, naturally."

Harvey plummeted from the rope to the floor and lumbered toward the others, squinting one eye and dragging one leg. He gave Olive a clumsy bow. "Mademoiselle," he mumbled.

"Come along, Quasimodo," said Horatio, turning back toward the stairs with a sweep of his green tail. "If we want to return home before it gets too dark, we had better be on our way."

The upstairs hallway was quiet, with only the distant murmur of Mr. and Mrs. Dunwoody's voices floating up from below. The silvery lake and the moonlit forest flickered softly in their canvases. All along the hall, glints traveled over the gilded frames, brightening and fading away.

"All clear, miss," Leopold murmured as Olive straightened the spectacles on her nose.

They climbed swiftly into the painting of Linden Street.

"Fascinating," Rutherford whispered as they hurried up the row of deserted front yards. "There's Mr. Fergus's house. That side must have been entirely remodeled since this painting was completed. And there's the Butlers'! I wonder why—" Rutherford's toe bumped an acorn. It skittered a few paces along the deserted street before wheeling back again. *"Fascinating!"* Rutherford interrupted himself. "I wonder if that acorn would return to its original spot at the same speed no matter how hard I kicked it!"

Rutherford was still kicking at acorns when they reached the walkway to the tall gray house. On the porch, a boy in a white nightshirt stood with his arms folded, scowling down at them.

"Happy Halloween, Morton!" called Olive.

"You look funny," said Morton.

"It's my costume." Olive approached the porch steps. "We're all in costumes."

Morton's frown deepened. "What is *that* supposed to be?" he asked, nodding toward Horatio.

Muttering something inaudible, Horatio attempted to hide himself in a patch of long grass.

"I'm a jabberwocky, so he's a mome rath," said Olive. "See his snout?"

Morton's round, pale face turned back toward Olive. "That's not very scary," he said. "I thought you were supposed to look scary for Halloween."

"*You're* going to be the scary one," said Olive. She pulled Morton's costume from its hiding spot beneath her sweatshirt.

Layers of the McMartins' ancient tablecloths fluttered eerily toward the ground. The delicate sheets were stitched together at the top and tattered at the bottom. Between the layers, Olive had dabbed tiny pictures in glow-in-the-dark paint, so that skeletons and jack-o'-lanterns and monstrous faces flickered through the fabric, like lanterns in a lacy mist.

"Golly," Morton breathed. He reached out one finger to touch the costume. "How does it glow like that?"

"I used glow-in-the-dark paint," said Olive, smiling proudly. "And if you have this costume covering you up, you can come out with us and do everything we do. You can go trick-or-treating, and walk around the neighborhood, and come to our school carnival, and nobody will notice a thing."

Morton's eyebrows rose. He gave the costume another careful poke.

"Here," said Olive. "I'll help you put it on."

"That is very clever," said Rutherford as Olive made Morton's eyes meet up with his costume's eyeholes. "It will keep your painted skin safe from both natural and artificial light, on top of disguising you very effectively. No one will notice how strange you look up close."

Morton's eyes narrowed. "You look strange from *far away.*"

"I hate to interrupt this cheery reunion," said Horatio, "but we ought to be on our way before Olive's parents notice our absence." He headed toward the street, muttering grumpily to himself. ". . . Although why you humans have decided to celebrate all that is dark and wicked by dressing up in ridiculous costumes and gorging yourselves on candy is beyond my comprehension."

Rutherford darted after the cat. "Well," he began, "the origins of Halloween, or All Hallows' Eve, date back to . . ."

The rest of the group hurried after them.

In the downstairs entryway, Olive made sure that every inch of Morton's paint-streaked skin was cloaked by his costume. She tucked the spectacles on their ribbon back inside her collar and glanced around at her friends. A faint flutter, half fear, half excitement, stirred in the bottom of her stomach.

"Mom! Dad!" she called down the hallway. "We're leaving!"

Mr. and Mrs. Dunwoody's smiling faces appeared around the edge of the kitchen door.

"Oh, don't you all look marvelous!" Mrs. Dunwoody exclaimed, bustling closer.

"Very frightening," Mr. Dunwoody agreed. "Rutherford, are you supposed to be an IRS agent?"

"I'm a professor of medieval history," said Rutherford.

"Oh, yes, of course," said Mr. Dunwoody. "The blazer. I should have known."

"And this is our friend Morton," said Olive, gesturing to the hooded ghost. "He lives . . . nearby."

"Very nice to meet you, Morton," said Mrs. Dunwoody.

The ghost held out a sheet-covered hand.

"All right, everyone, hold still for a quick photo!" said Mr. Dunwoody, raising the camera. "Move a bit closer together. Morton, turn fifteen degrees to your right. Olive, grab Horatio, would you? He seems to be trying to hide. Now give me your scariest poses. Say 'supernatural numbers'!"

"Supernatural numbers!"

The camera flashed.

* * * * *

Outside the old stone house, afternoon had dwindled into evening. The porch swing groaned softly on its chains. The ferns whispered to each other like watchful neighbors. Along the street, where the *real* neighbors usually watched and whispered, smiling pumpkins flickered on stoops, and golden lights glowed through open doorways. A few sparse clusters of children—more children than Olive had ever seen on Linden Street—scurried from door to door. As Olive watched from the top of the porch steps, one group of undersized pirates reached the path to the old stone house. They paused, their eyes traveling across the overgrown lawn to the chilly stone walls and darkly glimmering windows, up and up and up to the black peaks of the rooftops, where the branches of the trees rattled and scratched like skeletal hands.

The pirates ran away so fast that one of them lost his clip-on earring.

"Mom and Dad may have overestimated the number of trick-or-treaters they'll get," said Olive.

Morton stood beside her on the porch's worn floorboards. The breeze made his costume shift and shimmer, the painted faces grinning out at the street before hiding themselves again. His eyes traveled left, toward the upper floors of the old Nivens house—still dark, still gray, and still deserted—that loomed above the lilac hedge.

"It changed again," he said. "Last time, it was summer. Everything keeps changing." He kicked a dry leaf that had landed on the porch floor. It skittered down the steps and caught a rising draft of wind, sailing away over the lawn and out of sight. With the toe of the white sneakers that Olive had lent him, Morton gave the porch railing a kick. His shoe left a smudge that didn't fade away. Morton let out a laugh. "Let's go!" he shouted, hopping down the steps.

"Let's head to the right, and then loop around and proceed down the street," said Rutherford, following him. "That way we can visit the greatest number of houses without backtracking."

"An excellent stratagem, sir," said Leopold, striding after, with Harvey shuffling and squinting behind.

With her toes poised at the edge of the step, Olive felt a shudder twitch through her body. The hair on the back of her neck started to prickle. Suddenly the purplish sky seemed too dark, the air too chilly, the big house behind her too quiet, as if it were holding its breath, waiting for her to go away. She glanced down at Horatio.

"The house will be safe while we're gone, won't it?" she asked.

"This house is secure, Olive," Horatio answered. "Spells guard it; protection surrounds it. Besides, everything that Annabelle wants is out here." Olive swallowed hard as the cat's green eyes traveled from the spectacle-shaped bump under her collar down to the sidewalk, where Leopold and Harvey were marching and lumbering along. "As long as we all stay together, we should be safe."

Olive nodded. "I want Morton to have a real Halloween," she said. "I'm not going to let the McMartins take one more thing away." She watched the glowing ghost bounce impatiently up and down on the sidewalk. A little bit of Morton's excitement seemed to flutter back to her, like a summer breeze winding through a cool autumn night. "Let's go trick-or-treating!" she said, rushing down the steps with Horatio beside her.

They wound their way up and down the street, keeping far away from the empty windows of the Nivens house. Mr. Hanniman was giving out candy necklaces. The Butlers had SweeTarts and Skittles. Mr. Fergus was distributing granola bars, but at least they were the kind with chocolate chips. All the neighbors exclaimed over Olive's creative costume, and Morton's scary costume, and the cats' adorable costumes, and then asked what Rutherford was supposed to be.

"Perhaps I should have carried my encyclopedia of the Middle Ages," Rutherford said to Olive, after explaining the significance of his blazer for the tenth time.

"When we're done, you can have all of my candy,

Olive," said Morton loudly, bumping Rutherford off the sidewalk.

"Well, we're not done yet," said Olive. "Don't forget about the carnival!"

"The carnival!" Morton exclaimed, running ahead, with Harvey gallumphing at his heels. "The carnival!"

Morton's anticipation was contagious. Olive could feel it fizzing through her like bubbles in a just-opened bottle of pop, making everything seem lighter. But she couldn't get careless now, she reminded herself. It was up to her to keep an eye on everyone else. Above them, the purple sky was deepening to black. The moon, like a sliver of sharpened bone, slit the trails of passing clouds. If a living painting was going to creep up on them, now would be its perfect chance—when the night would hide them all, and the familiar houses of Linden Street were dwindling into the distance. Olive cast a glance over her shoulder. For a moment, the rooftop of the old stone house pierced through the net of black-branched trees. Then the group turned a corner, and the last trace of the house disappeared from sight.

"We just need to stay in busy areas," said Rutherford. Olive gave a little jump, startled that Rutherford had read her thoughts so clearly. "There are witnesses all around us," he went on. "We'll be safe."

Rutherford was right. The closer they got to the junior high, the more crowded and noisy the darkening streets became. By the time they reached the last block, they were being carried along on a steady stream of kids in costumes. The cats hissed at a pack of werewolves. Rutherford was smooshed against a glittery red devil. Olive found herself sandwiched between a headless horseman and a tall gray ghoul.

She glanced up into the ghoul's tattered hood. Hidden inside was a crumbling pit where a nose should have been, lips that shriveled back from yellowing teeth, and two sagging black sockets with living eyes glimmering in their depths.

Olive looked quickly away again.

Ahead of them, the junior high was lit up like a giant brick jack-o'-lantern. Warm yellow light and bursts of music streamed from its open doors. For the first time ever, the sight of school filled Olive with a rush of comfort.

"Listen, everyone," she said softly, urging the group into a huddle just outside the front doors. "They don't usually allow pets inside, so you three cats will have to be careful not to let any grown-ups see you."

"Don't worry, Olive," Horatio murmured. "We can be discreet. At least, *two* of us can." He shot a look at Harvey, who was sweeping a hunchbacked bow to a girl in a Gypsy costume.

As it turned out, Olive didn't need to worry about the cats being noticed. The crowd inside the front hall was so dense, three costumed hippopotami could have gone undetected. Strands of spiderweb trailed across the ceiling. Twists of black crepe paper threaded the warm air, where the smells of popcorn and caramel mingled in a sugary fog. Olive was jostled and shoved and bumped along, trying to keep her goggles firmly on her head and her feet firmly beneath her body.

"Remember to stay together!" she called over the noise.

But she was calling to no one.

OLIVE STARED AROUND the teeming school hallway. Rutherford, Morton, and the cats had vanished into the crowd like five raindrops into a river.

Olive felt a sickening jolt. They had to stay together.
Alone, each one of them would be vulnerable; each
one could become a target. She pressed one tent-
pegged hand over the lump of the spectacles. At least
they were still with her. Craning around for any sign of
the others, Olive let herself be carried along, through
the gymnasium doors.

There, the noise and color of the hall seemed to
explode outward, swelling and dimming like a burst
firework. The lights hanging from the ceiling had been
draped in layers of black and purple tissue, filling the
room with a violet haze. The wooden floor gleamed

like a mirror. Where the bleachers usually stood, rows of tents and tables flickered with false candle-light. Masked faces shifted around her. Nylon wings poked her in the sides. Robots and aliens bumped past, making muffled zapping noises with their plastic laser guns. And one tall gray ghoul loomed over her shoulder, coming just close enough to catch the corner of her eye.

Olive edged away from the ghoul's lurking figure. How come she couldn't find any of her friends, but she couldn't seem to lose one stranger?

"Rutherford?" she called, her voice useless against the carnival's roar. "Morton?"

She dodged through the crowd. If she could just find an open spot, or something tall to stand on, maybe she could get a clearer view and—

"Braaaaains?" intoned a low voice in her ear.

Olive whipped around and nearly planted her nose in a platter of pinkish gray goop. The goop looked suspiciously like molded Jell-O, and the zombie holding it looked suspiciously like her science teacher, but Olive's heart gave a little shiver anyway. It gave another, harder shiver a moment later, when the zombie shuffled to one side, revealing the tall gray ghoul just a few steps away.

Was it *following* her?

With a burst of panic, Olive raced to the left,

toward a massive display of carved pumpkins. Safe in their glow, she paused, breathing hard, and squinted into the nearby faces.

There was no one that she recognized . . . No one but the tall gray ghoul that came gliding slowly through the crowd, its hooded face swiveling to find her.

An imaginary hand grabbed Olive by the throat. She dove behind a knot of vampires drinking blood-colored sodas. Crouching close to the floor and keeping one eye fixed over her shoulder, Olive scuttled sideways, not noticing the tall black object in her path until she had crab-walked directly into it.

The tall black object turned around.

"Well, hello there," said Ms. Teedlebaum, squinting down at Olive. "Happy Halloween!"

"Um . . . happy Halloween," Olive managed.

The art teacher was dressed in black from head to toe, with rows and rows of silver chains wrapped tightly around her neck. Her kinky red hair had been combed straight up, so that it jutted like a petrified tassel from the top of her head. Its tips were splattered with glossy blots of orange paint.

"I'm a paintbrush," Ms. Teedlebaum announced. "I think it's perfectly obvious, but people keep asking."

"Oh," said Olive, glancing away just long enough to see that the ghoul had sunk back into the sea of costumes. "How—how did you—"

"Get my hair to stand up like this?" Ms. Teedle-baum supplied. "That's the other thing people keep asking. I used wood glue."

"Oh," said Olive. "Will that wash out?"

Ms. Teedlebaum paused. "To be honest, I didn't think that far ahead." She shrugged, smiling again. The rows of silver chains jangled. "I guess we'll see!"

Olive nodded.

"And what about you? Are you a cockroach?" Ms. Teedlebaum asked, gazing at Olive's goggles and scaly brown suit.

"I'm a jabberwocky. Like in *Alice in Wonderland*."

"Ah." Ms. Teedlebaum nodded. "I think I would prefer a cockroach infestation to a jabberwocky infestation, wouldn't you, Alice? But I'd prefer a butter-fly infestation to either of those. Why are there never infestations of *nice* things, I wonder." Shaking her head thoughtfully, the red-haired paintbrush wandered away.

Olive turned in a wobbly circle, trying to bring her brain back to the present. The ghoul was still nowhere to be seen—but neither were Rutherford, Morton, or the cats. Shrieks from the Haunted Maze shot through the sugary air, making Olive twitch. She clenched her hands inside the bulky gloves.

Rutherford and the cats could find their own way home. But what if she had lost Morton for good? What if he used this chance to run away from the house, from Elsewhere, and from Olive? Or what if he came too close to those flickering jack-o'-lanterns, and the candle flames caught the edge of this costume, and—

No, Olive told herself. That wasn't likely. It was much *more* likely that the McMartins would use this chance to separate them all, to scare and confuse them, and then to spring upon them, like wolves on a scattering herd of sheep. She had to find her friends again, before someone *else* did.

Olive stood on her tiptoes, searching the throng. *Please,* she thought. *Please, please, please.* And as though she had wished it into existence, a delicate greenish light, like the glimmer of a firefly, glowed through a seam in the crowd.

Olive's heart leaped.

"Excuse me," she murmured, darting past turtles and space troopers and someone dressed as a dachshund in a hotdog bun. She had to keep that firefly glow in sight. "Excuse me. Excuse me."

Two giggling fairies bounced past, knocking Olive off course. "Hey!" shouted the dark-haired fairy. She squinted at Olive, her glittery green eyeliner sparkling in the dimness. "You came as a *bat!*"

"Ew! Don't let it get caught in your hair!" squeaked the other fairy, and the two of them fluttered away, shrieking and covering their heads.

Olive spun around, trying to find the green light again, and felt something damp brush the side of her neck. Something slick and soft and almost rotten. She halted, looking up.

The tall gray ghoul loomed above her.

Letting out a gasp that no one heard, Olive stumbled backward through the crowd. The ghoul's eyes, two glinting black pits in the shade of its hood, glided after her. She dropped to her hands and knees, veering left and then right and then left again, putting as many other bodies as she could between herself and the thing in the rotten gray robes. When she was sure she'd lost it, she bolted toward the greenish glow of Morton's costume, weaving through the crowd until suddenly she could make out the familiar shapes of Morton, Rutherford, and all three cats, gathered around the mouth of an Egyptian tomb.

Olive skidded to a halt before the tomb's cardboard walls.

"There you are!" she panted, grabbing Morton's ghostly arm. "I was so—"

"Mademoiselle!" Harvey bellowed from the corner of his mouth. "You are safe!"

"Shh!" hissed Horatio, giving Harvey a warning swat on the head.

"What did you say?" Harvey bellowed even more loudly. "The cathedral bells have made me deaf!"

"*Shh!*" Horatio hissed again, pressing his green nose to Harvey's splotchy one.

"I thought I wouldn't find you again," Olive gasped, gazing around at all of them. "I thought something might already have happened to you."

"We were right here the whole time," said Morton, rather grumpily. He nodded at Rutherford. "This boy has been staring at the same display *forever*."

"I am almost certain that these hieroglyphs are gibberish," Rutherford observed, glancing up from a painted cardboard column. "And even I—who am *not* an expert on ancient Egypt—know that mummy cases were placed horizontally inside of sarcophagi, not left standing up so that mummies could reach out and attack nearby people," he added as the case swung open and a bandaged arm reached out to paw at the air.

"Listen, everyone," said Olive, lowering her voice to a whisper. "I think someone is *following* us."

"Whom do you mean, miss?" Leopold asked, stiffening.

Horatio's green eyes sharpened. "What makes you think so?"

Olive huddled against the tomb's cardboard corner. "I should have known," she whispered to the others. "It looked too tall and too *real* to be a kid in a costume." She pointed into the crowd. "Do you see that tall gray ghoul, right—"

But the towering hooded head wasn't there.

It wasn't anywhere.

Olive turned back to her friends. "I don't know where it went," she said. "It was right behind me when I came into the gym. And then . . ."

The words shriveled in Olive's throat.

On the silvery wooden floor, just behind the model tomb, lay a tattered slip of gray cloth. Olive's eyes traveled upward, along the tomb's wall, and came to rest on a hand—a bony, gray-skinned, rotten hand, with its long fingers wrapped around the wall's cardboard edge.

"Run!" she screamed.

Olive streaked toward the closest exit, a pair of doors that led not to the crowded front corridor, but to one of the school's inner halls. She smacked through the doors, their heavy panels creaking open to let out the many running feet that came right behind her. Everyone shot out into the dark corridor, the cats racing protectively around Olive's ankles, Morton reaching up to grab her gloved hand.

They turned a corner into an even darker hall. Beneath their footsteps and her own gasping breath, Olive could hear the gym doors creaking open, releasing a blast of screams and laughter before whooshing shut again.

. . . Leaving one more pair of footsteps to follow them into the darkness.

5

NO PLACE IS as silent as an empty school.

Even in the daytime, when all the lights were on and the sun was shining through the windows, Olive couldn't find her way around the junior high. Now, in the echoing darkness, she made one terrified turn after another. Her goggles slipped irritatingly over her eyes. Her heart smacked against her ribs. Panic pushed her forward like a cold, heavy hand.

"I think we need to turn *the other* way, Olive," said Rutherford, puffing in the blackness beside her.

"I believe he is correct, miss," Leopold added. "We ought to retrace our steps and return to the gymnasium, in order to—"

"We *can't* turn around," Olive argued. "That thing is right behind us! We need to find someplace to hide!"

They reached a spot where two hallways met, forming a knot of even thicker darkness. Olive halted, unsure of which way to go. Her heartbeat thundered in her ears—and still, beneath its pounding, she could hear the rustle of footsteps coming closer.

"This way. Quickly," Horatio commanded, bounding to the right.

Olive forced her legs back to a run.

They turned into another hallway, where a carpet of moonlight unrolled along the tiles beneath their feet. Olive glanced up, catching sight of the moon's bony hook gleaming through the high windows, and looked down again just in time to see Horatio dart through a gap in the hallway walls. Everyone else rushed after him.

Olive took a hasty look around. They were inside a stairwell, where a flight of steps disappeared into the darkness above. The cats crouched in the doorway, out of sight of the hall. Morton's robes flickered from the corner. Beneath the rhythm of her own heart, she could hear Rutherford's muffled breathing. For several seconds, there was no other sound.

"I believe we lost it," Leopold murmured at last.

There was another moment of silence.

Then Morton whispered, "Who do you think it is?"

Rutherford had an instant answer. "Well, it can't be Aldous McMartin, unless Annabelle found some way to get him out of his portrait on her own, which is highly unlikely. It could be Annabelle herself, or someone in her employ who she sent after us. Or, I suppose, it might not be a costume at all."

Morton's eyes were the size of billiard balls. "What do you mean? You mean that thing is a real ghost?"

"There's no such thing as ghosts," said Olive, giving Rutherford a hard look.

Rutherford blinked. The three cats turned to stare at Olive, their eyes glimmering like stained glass.

"Maybe it's just a high school student," Olive went on. "Or some other kid trying to scare us."

"What did you say?" Harvey blared. "'Bells on high ringing through Paris'?"

"Shh!" Horatio hissed.

Everyone fell silent.

Olive held her breath. There was no noise from the hallway outside. On her hands and knees, Olive edged out of the stairwell and squinted along the dim corridor. A few yards away, just inside the alcove of a locked classroom door, she could make out the edge of a rotting gray robe.

"It's still out there, just waiting for us!" she whispered, ducking back into the stairwell. "We can't stay here!"

With Olive leading the way, they scrambled up the flight of stairs into yet another deserted hall. Posters for the Halloween carnival fluttered like spectral leaves as they rushed past. Olive dropped the sack full of candy that was crinkling much too noisily on her arm, and she heard the smacks of Rutherford and Morton letting go of theirs as well. Spilled candy clattered on the tiles.

"We shouldn't have done this," Olive panted to the others. "I'm sorry. I thought we would be safe, if we—"

"We *will* be safe, if we can just outrun it," Leopold promised. "Follow me, men. And lady."

The black cat veered to the right, toward an open set of doors. They plunged through the archway, following a flight of steps down, down, down, into a long and windowless passage.

"Where are we?" Olive asked Rutherford, who was gasping in the blackness beside her.

"I have no idea," Rutherford answered. "And you know that I do not use those words, in that particular combination, often."

"Is that thing still coming after us? Can you hear its thoughts?"

"As I don't even know who or what it *is*," Rutherford huffed, "I would have to stop and stare directly into its eyes in order to get a clear reading, and I find that thought rather unappealing."

"Halt!" said Leopold, before Olive could ask another question. "We seem to have reached an impasse."

Olive groped through the blackness. A smooth, solid surface sealed off the end of the corridor. This was a dead end. "Oh no," she breathed. *"No."* She gave the wall a desperate shove. Before them, the solid surface swung forward, sending the groan of disused hinges echoing through the passageway.

"It's another door!" Olive shouted. "Come on!"

Everyone stumbled through the doorway into a vast, open space. It was far too dark to see the room's dimensions, but the smacks of their footsteps reverberated against a ceiling that hung high above their heads, and the air felt cool and still. Rows of tiny white bulbs formed wide stripes along the floor. In the distance, one red light hung high on the wall, tingeing the darkness with a bloody haze.

"Are we still in your school?" Morton whispered.

Olive frowned around at the dim white lights. She took another step forward, and her knee nudged the first seat in a row that curved away into the darkness.

"I know where we are!" she called to the others. "We're in the auditorium!"

"Olive, are you *trying* to let our pursuer know exactly how to find us?" hissed Horatio from the vicinity of Olive's shins. "We ought to find another way out of here, before . . ." Horatio's whiskers twitched. His ears flicked back, catching a trace of sound.

A split second later, Olive heard it too: the rusty groan of the passage doors.

The ghoul had followed them into the auditorium.

Behind the towering creature, the passage doors thumped softly shut. For a moment, the ghoul kept still, its hooded face turning from one of them to the other, taking in the cats, the dimly glowing ghost, the miniature professor, and the petrified jabberwocky in sweatpants. Olive knew just what Horatio had been about to say: They needed to find another way out, before they were trapped here. Alone. Far from the crowd, and the lights, and the teachers, and the exits. Just like they were trapped now.

Silence hung in the air like a blade about to fall.

And then several things happened at once.

"Run!" screamed Olive.

"Men, split up!" yelled Harvey.

"Men, stay together!" yelled Leopold.

"The light booth!" shouted Rutherford.

"The outer doors!" shouted Horatio.

"Olive!" screamed Morton.

At the explosion of sound, the ghoul gave a start, staring around as its prey darted in all directions.

Rutherford shot up one aisle. Horatio took another. Leopold and Harvey charged off into the rows of seats. Grabbing a wad of Morton's sleeve, Olive hauled him toward the dim red light, which cast its glow over the steps that led to the stage.

Black boards thudded under their feet. Dragging Morton behind her, Olive rushed toward the stage's closed curtains. There had to be a stage door on the other side. But there seemed to be no gap in the heavy black velvet, and another set of steps was crossing the stage, drawing closer and closer. The tremor of the floorboards threaded upward into her spine—

—and, with a sudden, audible *clunk,* every light in the room went out.

Without the spokes of white along the floor or the red glow of the work light, the air in the auditorium was as black as a jar full of ink.

"Olive?" whispered a voice from over her shoulder—a voice that *wasn't* Morton's.

Olive wheeled around just as a beam of light, bright and pure as a pillar of ice, speared through the darkness and shattered across the stage.

Morton let out a shriek.

Half blinded, shielding her face with one arm, Olive blinked into the blue-white glare. Inches away from her, near enough that she could have reached out and touched its rotting gray robes, stood the ghoul. It too was wavering and blinking into the light.

"Everybody freeze!" shouted Rutherford's voice from the light booth, where the giant spotlight was aimed at the stage.

Nobody listened.

Morton had already flopped down and wormed his way under the hem of the curtains, away from the burning white beam. The cats leaped from the rows of seats up onto the stage, forming a protective barricade around Olive's shins. Olive backed up until her wire wings caught in the curtains.

Only the ghoul stood still.

Its skeletal frame was bathed in the light. Olive imagined its knobby hand reaching up and pulling back that hood, revealing a heap of long, dark hair, and a pair of pretty, icy, painted eyes. But it wasn't dissolving, as the living portraits of Annabelle or Aldous would have.

In fact, it seemed to be *shivering*.

Olive wriggled her wings free of the curtain and took one tiny step forward. From the sunken pits of the ghoul's face, two wide blue eyes watched her warily.

"Take off that mask," she commanded.

The ghoul reached up with two bony hands. There was a sound like a rubber band stretching, and then the mask and hood were gone, leaving only a very skinny, very tall, very young man—a young man with stringy red hair, bulbous blue eyes, and a nervous expression—to stare back at her.

"Who are you?" Olive demanded.

The young man's mouth worked from side to side, as though the answer had gotten stuck in his teeth. He hunched his shoulders around his long, skinny neck. He cleared his throat with a startlingly deep rumble.

"Walter," he said, in a very, very low voice.

"Why are you following us?"

"Mmm. Because I'm—um—" Walter swallowed, and Olive could see his Adam's apple bobbing up and down in his scrawny neck. "Because I'm your bodyguard."

"YOU'RE *WHAT?*" SAID Olive. Walter drew his head even closer to his shoulders and folded his lanky arms across his chest. "I'm your bodyguard," he repeated, in a deep, slow voice.

Pressed against Olive's legs, the three cats fluffed their fur and made themselves as large and important as possible. Harvey forgot he was supposed to be a hunchback, and stood up like a stuffed cat in a museum. Leopold looked so tightly inflated that Olive feared the tip of one of her wings might pop him.

"She already *has* a guard," snapped Horatio. "Three of them, in fact."

Walter looked surprisingly unsurprised by the talking cat. "These are the familiars," he rumbled. "I've heard about them."

"Wait," said Olive, before too many more questions could pile up and crush her first one. "What do you mean, you're my bodyguard?"

Walter's knobby shoulders shifted. "Mmm . . . I was supposed to follow you," he began. His voice was so deep that it seemed to be coming from someplace a few floors below his body. "I was supposed to watch. Make sure you were safe. I wasn't supposed to scare you. You weren't even supposed to know." Walter paused, his eyes darting anxiously from one of them to another. "But you kept running away. So I had to run after you. And now . . ." Walter kneaded the hollow ghoul's mask in both hands. "Mmm," he grumbled deep in his throat. "Now my aunt's going to be so mad."

"Your aunt?" Olive echoed.

Walter's eyes widened. "I wasn't supposed to tell you. They're trying to stay undercover."

" 'They'?"

"Oh, no." Walter closed his eyes. "Could you—mmm—could you turn off that light? It's hard to think."

There was another *clunk* from the light booth. The spotlight clicked off, the floor lights blinked on, and Rutherford emerged into the aisle, leaving one row of houselights glowing dimly behind him.

"You're Rutherford Dewey," said Walter as Rutherford hurried down the aisle. "And that's the Nivens boy. The one trapped in the painting," he added, nodding at the lump behind the curtains.

Morton's head poked out from behind the velvet, his eyes glaring at Walter beneath his lifted hood.

"Well," said Olive, "since you seem to know everything about us, it might be fair if you told us a little about *you.*"

Walter sighed a deep, rumbling sigh. He rubbed his head with the empty mask, making his hair stand up in uneven reddish spikes. "Mmm . . ." he said again, looking so uncomfortable under everyone's scrutiny that Olive almost felt sorry for him. But not quite.

"I belong to a group that opposes dark magic," Walter began at last. "The S-M-U-D-S."

"The Smuds?" said Rutherford. He stood at the edge of the stage, staring intently at Walter's face.

"The—mmm—the Society of Magicians United against—mmm—Dark Spells," Walter explained. "I'm a junior member. Sort of. Or an apprentice. Almost." He blinked at Rutherford. "That's how I know your grandmother. And we know about all of you." His eyes fluttered over the rest of them.

"Are you here because of the increased threat from the McMartins?" Rutherford asked.

Walter nodded. "We know what's been happening in their house. But we were supposed to stay undercover. If you didn't know we were watching the house, then—mmm—then the McMartins might not know either."

"We thought *you* were Annabelle," said Morton angrily, crawling out from the curtains to stand beside Olive.

"Or something Annabelle had summoned," Olive added.

"No," said Walter. "I'm just a dope whose aunt is going to yell at him." Head bowed, he glanced around at the circle of wary faces. "Can I—can I at least escort you home?"

Leopold's chest inflated even further. "We do not require an additional escort," he huffed.

"No. I know you don't." Walter's deep voice softened. "Mmm . . . I just meant I could go *with* you. Safety in numbers."

Leopold gave a puffy harrumph.

"What do you think, Rutherford?" Olive asked.

Rutherford nodded slowly. "I think Walter is telling the truth," he said.

"Very well," said Horatio. His eyes gave Walter a last sharp scan. "Then let us return to the house. Some of us would rather *not* spend the night attired in green paint and plastic snouts."

A jabberwocky, a ghost, a professor, three cats, and one tall gray ghoul wound their way back through the junior high school and out the open front doors. The cats kept a watchful eye on Walter, Olive noticed, but once the group had passed through the school doors, they turned most of their attention back to the dark lawns and quiet streets.

Morton hadn't said a word since they'd left the auditorium. The paint in his costume had faded to a mild green glow, and he kept his eyes fixed on the sidewalk. Olive wasn't sure if it was the prospect of going home, or the fact that the night had been far more frightening than fun that was dampening Morton's mood. Maybe she didn't *want* to know. There was nothing she could do about either of those things now. Still, she stuck close to Morton, keeping several feet of space between herself and the flapping edges of Walter's long gray robes. She wasn't sure what to think of Walter yet—but if Rutherford saw no reason to doubt him, then there was nothing in his mind to earn their distrust.

Rutherford, in fact, was acting downright *friendly.*

"But that is the problem with dressing up as a dinosaur, of course," he opined to Walter as a cold rush of wind swept along the sidewalk, battering them with a swirl of dry leaves. "There are so many potential inaccuracies. Benjamin Davis's costume seemed to imply that a Tyrannosaurus rex had five-fingered claws and a zipper along its spine. *Highly* implausible."

"Mmm," said Walter agreeably.

"Of course, dinosaurs are one of my areas of semi-expertise," Rutherford went on. "What about you? What types of magic have you been studying? Are you an expert on any particular methods or subjects?"

"Mmm . . ." said Walter. "Well, I'm interested in conjuration. But my aunt doesn't think I have the gift. She's a messenger," he added, a hint of admiration lightening his deep voice. "She can communicate with the dead. And she says . . . mmm . . . She says they don't have any messages for me." Walter paused for a moment. "That means I won't succeed at anything hard. So I've been learning basic spells. Protection. Summoning. Mmm. Stuff like that."

"So have I!" said Rutherford. "What do you think of substituting Picklox for Hookweed in a basic keyhole spell? Of course, it's not authentic to the spell's medieval roots, but . . ."

They turned the final corner, and Olive's mind traveled away from Rutherford and Walter and Morton to hurry up the slope of Linden Street.

The trick-or-treaters had vanished as suddenly as they'd appeared. Here and there, the nub of a candle continued to sputter behind a pumpkin's fading smile. Most of the neighbors had switched off their porch lights, leaving their houses dark and unwelcoming.

But none of them were quite as dark and unwelcoming as the Nivens house.

Morton's older sister, Lucinda—the closest thing to a friend that Annabelle McMartin had ever had—had lived for decades in that quiet gray house, hiding her painted skin from the daylight, keeping its rooms spotless and its garden neat. Now clusters of crabgrass sprouted in the cracks of the walkway. Thistles and creeping vines invaded the once-perfect rose beds. Grass and weeds grew high around its walls, as though they were trying to help the house itself to disappear.

When they reached its walkway, Morton stopped so abruptly that Rutherford, who had been rattling off a list of medieval herbs, smacked directly into him.

"Someone's in there," Morton whispered.

"What are you talking about?" Olive followed Morton's eyes toward the silent gray house. In one upper window, where the pane of glass had been shattered, pale curtains twitched gently in the wind. "Oh, that? It's just a broken window, Morton."

"No." Morton shook his head. "There's someone in there." The cats stopped to cluster around them. Rutherford and Walter leaned closer. "I saw a light," Morton went on. "It *moved*."

Walter straightened up and gave the street a long, careful look. "This way," he said softly. "To the back."

Before anyone could question him, he had taken off across the overgrown lawn.

The rippling hem of Walter's costume made a

darker trail across the dewy grass. Dead leaves crackled beneath Olive's feet as she hurried after him,
with Rutherford, Morton, and the cats close behind.
They edged around the corner of the house, through
a clump of withered hydrangeas, into the shelter of
the house's back wall. Through the nearest windows,
Olive spotted a flicker of light—the faint, floating
glimmer of a candle gliding through the house's quiet
rooms.

She glanced down at Morton, but he wasn't looking
at her. He was watching Walter, who had stopped at
the back door, with one hand pressed against the wood.
Walter's voice was soft, but Olive caught the stream
of words it carried—words from some other language,
low and smooth and strange.

"Walter?" she breathed. "What are you doing?"

Walter didn't answer.

The door creaked open before them. A breath of
air drifted out of the darkness inside, cold and smoky
with the scent of dust. Somewhere in the depths of the
house, the glimmering light bobbed and brightened.

Walter stepped over the threshold.

Morton followed him.

"Morton, wait!" Olive whispered, darting after him
through the gaping doorway. The cats brushed against
her legs, keeping close.

Rutherford hurried behind. "I'm not sure this is

wise," Olive heard him say, before the door banged shut, leaving them all sealed in the dark.

Olive blinked around. She could feel one of the cats pressed against her leg, and she could see the dying glow of Morton's sleeve, but everything else was black. Walter's voice rumbled up from somewhere nearby, startling and dangerously near, like the thunder of an approaching storm.

"We're here," he called into the darkness.

"HUSH!" WHISPERED A VOICE.
Footsteps rustled through the dimness. The floating light drew nearer, its ruddy glow sliding along the hallway. When it reached the room where Olive and her friends stood, it tightened into the small, shifting flame of a candle, throwing its beams over the cabinets and countertops of Mrs. Nivens's deserted kitchen. There, the candle—and whoever was holding it—halted, too far away to be clearly seen.

"They noticed me," said Walter, shuffling toward the light.

"Oh, Walter," the distant voice sighed. "Why am I not surprised?" The candle flickered. "Come inside, all of you. And Walter—lock the door."

Morton stepped farther into the room, and Olive

came with him, still holding tight to his sleeve. The cats and Rutherford followed. Behind them, Walter turned the lock, its metal click loud and sharp in the stillness.

"There," said the voice, coming closer. Olive stared at the candlelit face that came with it. It had high, dramatic cheekbones, arching black eyebrows, and eyes that were a strange shade of silvery gray, as cool and changeable as mirrors.

"This is my aunt Delora," said Walter, trying to untangle his long arms from his costume's even longer sleeves. "Mmm—Aunt Delora, this is Olive Dunwoody and Rutherford Dewey and—"

"I know who they are," the woman interrupted, brushing one pale hand through the air as if she were waving away a trail of smoke. Her mirrory eyes landed on Olive. "I hope all of you feel as at home as I do in the darkness, enclosed in its soft embrace."

Actually, Olive felt quite the opposite about the darkness, but Walter's aunt wasn't waiting for an answer.

"Of course, some of us are more comfortable never being seen . . . in the flesh, as it were," Delora went on. Her eyes traveled away from Olive, back up into the sooty air. "Those of us who float between the worlds: What need have we for bodies at all?"

Horatio cocked one whiskery eyebrow. "Hands must

be rather useful for holding that candle," he muttered.

Olive gave him a little shove with the toe of her shoe.

Delora didn't seem to notice. "Please, come into the study," she said, swishing her pale hand through the air again. "There we can speak more freely." With a flutter of long black skirts, she trailed ahead of them into the hallway.

Olive glanced at Rutherford. He nodded.

They followed the blotch of candlelight along the narrow hall, the floorboards groaning softly under their feet. Walter, who had finally wormed his way out of the ghoul suit, lurched hurriedly after them.

Delora paused beside a closed door. A ribbon of rosy light slipped through the crack beneath it, widening and brightening as she opened the door and ushered them through.

Inside, Lucinda Nivens's formal dining room had been transformed into the strangest "study" that Olive had ever seen. In fact, it looked more like a laboratory that had collided with a graveyard while being rained on by a traveling carnival. Lucinda's spotless white chairs were draped with dark shawls and brocade blankets. Burning candles were wedged into bottles, jars, and the tops of a few yellowish skulls, which Olive hoped were made of plastic. A collection of old botanical diagrams were tacked haphazardly to the walls, and a row of bottles full of tinted liquids was arranged in a metal tray on the sideboard. A giant stuffed raven with red glass eyes stared down at the room from its perch on the curtain rod. Atop the long dining table, two antique oil lamps burned dully. The rest of the table's dark wooden surface was littered with stones and vials and beakers and loose papers and clumps of dirt and bunches of dried herbs. A gilt-framed hand mirror lay at one end, next to a deck of very strange-looking cards.

In the far corner of the room stood a desk. At the desk sat a bearded man in a worn brown suit. He got to his feet as the others came in. The man was large. His suit was not. As he crossed the room to greet them, Olive felt the urge to duck, in case one of his vest buttons should come shooting off and hit her in the eye.

"Welcome," said the man, taking Olive's hand between his large, damp palms. "Welcome. *Welcome.*" He shook Rutherford's and Morton's hands too, brushing at his hair and his jacket with compulsive little swipes in between. "Rutherford Dewey," he boomed, shaking Rutherford's hand for the second time. "I've heard all about you from your grandmother. The magical community expects great things. And *this,*" he added, turning back to the hooded ghost, "must be Morton Nivens, the century-old child. I've been fascinated by your family's story for quite some time."

Olive felt a zing of hope. "You have?" she broke in. "Do you know where Mary and Harold Nivens are?"

"Regrettably, no," said the bearded man. His eyes traveled back to Morton. "I don't suppose that you would remove that costume, so that I might—"

Morton grabbed his hood with both hands and pulled it tighter over his head. He hopped backward, out of the man's reach. The cats clustered protectively around him.

"And these are the McMartin familiars, of course," the man went on, smiling down at the glaring trio.

"We are no longer in the McMartins' service," said Horatio stiffly.

"No, of course not." The bearded man wheeled back to Olive. "And Olive Dunwoody—the ordinary little girl who is brave enough to live in a witches' den."

Olive wasn't sure that she liked this description of herself. The more she thought about it, the less sure she was.

"And who are *you?*" she asked as the man shook her hand for the third time, and the sleeve encasing his arm began to look dangerously strained.

"Do pardon my rudeness. I am Byron Widdecombe, expert on magical history, semi-expert on magical genealogy—dark magicians in particular."

Rutherford looked as though someone had lit a wick inside his head.

"*The* Byron Widdecombe?" he repeated, eyes wide. "Author of *A Dauntingly Dry Description of the Medieval Magician's Herbarium?*"

"The very same." The bearded man gave Rutherford a bow, and Olive was sure she could hear threads popping.

"I've been studying that book!" said Rutherford, beginning to jiggle from foot to foot. "I would like to discuss the various purposes you theorize that Witchnail might serve to—"

"Rutherford, wait," said Olive, grabbing him by the tweed sleeve. "Mr. Widdecombe, you said you're an expert on *dark* magicians? So you're a—"

"Oh, dear me, no," the man interrupted. He waved his meaty hands. "I am a *scholar* of dark craft, not a practitioner. My own magic is of the standard academic variety."

"Standard academic variety" didn't sound too threatening to Olive, whatever it meant. Still, she gave Rutherford a pointed look.

Rutherford blinked back at her. "He's telling the truth, Olive."

"Our only intention is to help you, Olive," said Delora, who had settled herself beside the funny-looking cards. Her silvery eyes fixed on Olive's face—or, rather, just above Olive's face, as though she were looking at something much more interesting that was floating over Olive's head.

Olive glanced up at the empty air.

"That is why my husband and I are here: To help you." Delora raised her graceful hands, gesturing around the room. Her eyes coasted over Walter, who was seated awkwardly on the edge of the table. "And Walter too, of course," she added, as an afterthought. "Walter is not a naturally talented witch, but he can at least keep watch over you and your home." Her eyes flicked up to the spot above Olive's head again, and Olive fought the urge to reach up and swat at the air. "I remain patient with him, in hopes that one day he will do *something* right."

Olive glanced at Walter. He perched on the very edge of the table, gazing straight down, with his bony legs reaching all the way to the floor. His narrow shoulders squirmed. His Adam's apple bobbed. He looked like a long-legged water bird trying to swallow a too-large fish.

Olive felt a sudden impulse to pat him on the head.

"If you would not object, Olive," the bearded man took over, "perhaps we could visit the house tomorrow. It might prove very helpful to our cause. Even as a historical artifact, it is of great scholarly interest."

"Oh . . . I don't know," said Olive. "My parents don't know the truth about the McMartins, and I'm not sure I should . . ."

"Say no more." The man waved his hands. "We shall wait for a more convenient time."

"When it is meant to happen, it will happen," Delora added, as though she were announcing a wise and important truth.

"Mr. Widdecombe," said Rutherford, who had been jiggling impatiently all this time.

"It's *Doctor* Widdecombe, actually," said *Doctor* Widdecombe.

"Doctor Widdecombe, may I ask what you are working on at the moment?"

"Besides keeping watch for the McMartins and protecting their familial home—my own spells are currently guarding the house from evil intentions, as it happens—and caring for my beloved Delora, whose gift makes her exceedingly sensitive to troubles of all kinds . . ." He turned toward Delora, who placed one hand over her forehead and closed her eyes. ". . . I am preparing a study on the speed at which various herbal extractions lose their potency."

"Fascinating," said Rutherford.

It sounded anything *but* fascinating to Olive. As Rutherford and Doctor Widdecombe discussed the row of glass bottles, and Delora rearranged her cards, and Walter rocked uneasily back and forth on the table, Olive let her eyes wander around the rest of the room. On the shelves that lined one wall, knick-knacks that must have belonged to Lucinda Nivens— or to Mary and Harold Nivens before her—had been pushed aside to make room for other, stranger objects. China cups and porcelain bud vases had been wedged into the corners, giving way to heavy leather books and bumpy brass binoculars and stoppered bottles. Also wedged into a corner, his arms folded, glowering out at all of them, was Morton. He had pushed his robes back at last, revealing his round and furious face.

Olive edged toward him. "Morton?" she asked, under her breath. "What's wrong?"

Morton's lips pressed each other into a flat, angry line. "They're in *my house*," he whispered.

"Well—sort of," Olive whispered back. "It used to be yours, and then it was Lucinda's for a while, and now it's sort of . . . no one's."

"It's *mine*," said Morton. "It's ours. It belongs to me and my parents." His voice grew louder with each word. "And we're going to need it *back*."

Rutherford and Doctor Widdecombe stopped speaking. Delora and Walter rose to their feet.

"These people are just using the house for a little while, Morton," said Olive, feeling a bit embarrassed. "They're helping to keep us safe."

"But *I* didn't say they could stay here. My mama and papa didn't say they could stay here, and move their stuff, and change everything, and push all the furniture around. And we're going to need this table, when—" Morton broke off.

When *what?* Olive wondered, watching him. Why would Morton and his long-lost, no-longer-living parents need a dining room table, here, in the real world?

Morton seemed to be wondering the same thing. The anger on his face trickled away like melting frost. He stared down at the rug.

Leopold leaned supportively against Morton's knees.

"Do you want to go home, Morton?" Olive asked, after one long, quiet moment. "To Elsewhere, I mean?"

Morton nodded. Still looking at the floor, he pulled his hood back over his face.

"I suppose Rutherford ought to be heading home as well," said Doctor Widdecombe, trying to sound jovial. "Mrs. Dewey will worry if he's too late. Tomorrow is Sunday, which I assume means no school for any of you. If you are free to visit us, Olive, please do. For now, a good Hallows' Eve to you all."

Walter guided them to the back door. He opened it wordlessly, waiting for them to step out. Olive glanced up into his face as she stepped over the threshold, but she couldn't tell whether the expression on it was anger, or humiliation, or something else entirely. The lock clicked behind them.

"It looks like your parents are waiting for you," said Rutherford, nodding toward the old stone house. Lights glowed from its downstairs windows, making the muffled darkness of the Nivens house seem even darker and lonelier by comparison. Rutherford gave them all a courtly bow. "Good night."

"Good night, Featherbird!" Harvey called after him, in Quasimodo's mumbly voice.

"Were you talking about Doctor Widdecombe and Delora when you said we wouldn't have to fight alone?" Olive asked Horatio as she followed his bushy tail through the lilac hedge. "Did you know they were here all along?"

"I was aware of their presence," Horatio answered, "and of their protective spells enclosing the house, of course. But secrecy was required."

"Hmmph," said Morton.

"How did you know?" Olive asked, pushing the lilac branches apart for Morton to wriggle through. "How come you can sense things that I don't even *notice*?"

Horatio paused to watch Olive untangle Morton's cuff from a knot of brittle twigs. "As I've told you, Olive, we cats can see things that others cannot."

Morton straightened up on the other side of the hedge. "Then why can't you see where Mama and Papa are?" he demanded.

"I'm afraid we cannot do *everything*," Horatio huffed. "We can only speak, and open doors, and move objects, and sense the presence of magic." He marched toward the front of the old stone house, throwing the words back over his shoulder. "Perhaps you would be more impressed if we juggled live mice while balancing teacups on our heads."

"Who hiccups under beds?" slurred Harvey, dragging his leg through the grass.

"Morton didn't mean that as an insult, Horatio," said Olive.

"Yes, I did!" said Morton.

"He *is* only a little boy," Leopold put in.

Morton stomped one foot. "I am *not* a little boy!"

"Well—" Olive began.

"I'm not!" Morton interrupted. "I may look like I'm nine years old, but I've been alive much longer than *you!*"

"Not longer than I," Harvey mumbled from the corner of his mouth. "I looked down from the rooftops of the great cathedral of Notre Dame to see the city of Paris built, stone by stone, and to watch—"

"He wasn't talking to *you,* you ninny," said Horatio. "Why don't you pretend to be deaf again?"

By the time they reached the front porch steps, everyone was arguing.

No one noticed that the jack-o'-lanterns had toppled over and rolled away beneath the creaking swing. No one noticed that although lights still burned behind the closed doors of the library and the parlor, all the entrance lights had been turned off, leaving the hallway in total darkness. Even when Olive opened the front door and led the group—now arguing in whispers—inside, no one noticed that the rug had been rumpled and shoved aside, or that the coat tree had fallen down, leaving a dent in the polished hardwood floor.

Not until Olive switched on the lights, illuminating trails of spilled candy and walls scuffed with the marks of kicking feet and clawing nails, did anyone notice that something in the old stone house had gone terribly, horribly wrong.

"Mom?" Olive called, venturing into the hallway. "Dad?"

Her toes hit something that glinted on the floorboards. Olive glanced down. It was a pair of glasses with thick lenses and bent wire frames. Her father's glasses. The glasses he never went anywhere without.

"Mom? Dad?" Olive shouted—though she already knew that there would be no answer.

FOR OLIVE, TIME stopped at that moment. Perhaps it went on for other people, whose watches kept ticking and whose hearts kept beating, but for Olive, the passing minutes fell away like links cut out of a chain. She couldn't feel, or see, or remember a thing until suddenly the gears seemed to catch again, and Mrs. Dewey was squeezing her against one silk-robed shoulder, and she was sitting on the bottom step of the staircase, with Morton two steps above her, and a pair of wire wings in her lap.

Olive glanced up. Curlers were clustered around Mrs. Dewey's head like a halo of pink mushrooms. Her robe smelled of lavender and several stranger spices, and her face was worried and warm.

"Are you sure you wouldn't like to drink this,

Olive?" she asked, holding up a small white bottle. "It will help you to feel less upset."

But Olive didn't want to feel less upset. An awful thing had just happened, and she wanted to feel every last bit of its awfulness. Anything else would be pretend.

"No," she said into Mrs. Dewey's squishy shoulder. "No, thank you."

"The cats are searching the house," said Rutherford. His voice sounded strangely slow to Olive, and his wiry body was unusually still. He stood beside the newel post, dressed in his blue dragon pajamas. "If there are any other clues to be found, I am certain that they will find them."

"It doesn't matter," Olive croaked. The lump in her throat seemed to grow larger each time she swallowed, and it hurt to squeeze the words out. "We already know who took my parents. And we know it's my fault."

For once, Rutherford said nothing. For the space of several seconds, there were only the sounds of Olive sniffling into Mrs. Dewey's soggy shoulder, and the bare trees tapping against the walls outside, stirred by gusts of autumn wind.

The quiet was smashed by a sudden knock at the front door. Rutherford hurried to open it. With a burst of chilly air, Doctor Widdecombe, Delora, and Walter blew through the doorway of the old stone house.

Doctor Widdecombe planted himself in the middle

of the entryway, letting the others squeeze in behind him. "Oh my," he said. "Oh my, my, my." From her damp spot on Mrs. Dewey's shoulder, Olive watched his eyes take in the long, dim hallway, the library's carved double doors, the scratched wooden paneling, and the glimmering paintings on each wall. "Oh my, my, *my*," he breathed.

Delora swayed behind him, wrapped up in a huge black shawl like a cross between a mummy and a vampire. "Yes," she whispered, closing her silvery eyes. "There is danger here. Powerful, deep-rooted darkness." Her eyelids fluttered open. "You poor child," she murmured, reaching out to stroke Olive's hair.

Olive leaned closer to Mrs. Dewey.

Walter towered behind his aunt and uncle. His mussed-up hair had been slicked tight to his skull, making his smallish head look like a pea on a pedestal. "What should we do?" he asked, pushing the sleeves of his sweater up his spindly arms. The sleeves slipped back down again. "Call the police?"

"Certainly *not*," said Doctor Widdecombe, glancing up from the scratches on the newel post. "These are matters that they would not understand."

"The cats and I shouldn't have left all at once," said Olive, rubbing her stinging eyes with her sweatshirt cuff. "I shouldn't have gone at all. But we thought the house was safe."

"We *all* thought the house was safe, Olive," Mrs.

Dewey assured her. "I used a charm against uninvited guests, Byron added his protective spells, Delora foresaw no reason to worry—"

Olive shook her head violently. "I should have known Annabelle would find a way inside," she said. "But I thought she would come after *me,* not my parents. I don't know what she'll do with them." Olive swallowed a sob. "What if we're already too late?"

Delora glided to the foot of the stairs. "I am quite certain that your parents are alive, Olive," she said. Her voice was soft and steady. "If they were not, I would hear them speaking from the other side. But if you have an object that belonged to one of them, something they used frequently, I may be able to tell you more . . ."

Olive sniffled. Slowly, she held out her father's glasses, which she'd been gripping so tightly that their lenses were white with fog.

Delora closed her eyes again, lifting the glasses on one palm. "I can see him," she murmured.

Olive held her breath.

"Yes . . ." Delora continued. "A tall, thin man . . . receding brown hair . . . a blue shirt with an ink stain on its sleeve . . ."

Olive's heart performed a pole vault. "That's what he was wearing tonight!" she exclaimed.

"That is all that I can see," said Delora, looking down at Olive. "But I can assure you, Olive, that he is most definitely alive."

Olive let out a burst of air. "What about my mother?" she asked, jumping to her feet. "Can you make sure about her too?" While everyone stared after her, Olive raced into the library, grabbing the silver pen that always lay at a perfect ninety-degree angle along the side of her mother's desk. She skidded back into the entryway and pressed the pen into Delora's hands.

Delora's eyelids fluttered. "I see the hands that held this pen. No polish on the nails. A wedding ring engraved with an infinity symbol—"

"That's her!" said Olive.

With a little smile, Delora put the pen and the glasses back into Olive's hands. "She too is still within the realm of the living."

Relief washed over Olive like a warm bath. She sank limply back down onto the step beside Mrs. Dewey. "Thank you," she whispered.

"What puzzles me, Doctor Widdecombe," said Rutherford, "is why Annabelle would have abducted Mr. and Mrs. Dunwoody while leaving Olive herself behind. On their own, they don't possess anything that Annabelle would want."

"Ah." Doctor Widdecombe folded his hands over his substantial belly. "But there is one obvious purpose for which she may have taken them."

Olive blinked up at Doctor Widdecombe. *Ingredients for spells?* suggested the panicky voice in the back of her brain. *Food for magical monsters?*

"Bargaining," said Doctor Widdecombe. "She will try to exchange them for something of value."

"You mean, 'Something *else* of value,'" said Mrs. Dewey.

"Yes," said Doctor Widdecombe. He wiped his hands on the front of his jacket. "Yes, of course."

Olive's hands shot to the spectacles tied under her collar. "Well—then—maybe I should just offer her what she wants," she said shakily. The spectacles seemed to prickle against her skin, like metal hit by a sudden frost. "Because what I want most of all is to have my mom and dad back."

Delora widened her silvery eyes. "Do not be too eager," she warned. "With our help, you may not need to give her anything at all."

"Delora is right, Olive," said Mrs. Dewey, patting Olive's shoulder. "If we can just be patient, Annabelle will eventually come to *us.*"

As the others spoke, Doctor Widdecombe strode slowly away down the hall. He examined each doorway and peered into each open room. The glow of the wall sconces slid over his belly, like acrobats trying to balance on a ball. "It seems likely that Annabelle would take other things while she had the opportunity," he said, staring into the silent parlor. "Is anything else of significance missing from the house, Olive? Any magical tools or objects? A book of family spells, perhaps?"

"I don't know yet," said Olive. "The cats are checking everywhere. Besides, Annabelle wants this whole *house* back."

"I find it astonishing that Annabelle was able to enter the house in spite of your spells, Doctor Widdecombe," said Rutherford, following the doctor's motions with worshipful eyes.

"As do I," Doctor Widdecombe answered. "As do I." He moved slowly toward the foot of the stairs, hands clasped behind his back. "Generally, an opponent must already be aware of the spells that have been cast in order to counteract them. This leaves us with two possibilities: Either Annabelle was expecting these *specific* spells and came to the house prepared to undo them . . . or her powers are somehow growing stronger."

Under the weight of these words, everyone fell silent.

Olive didn't know what the others were thinking, but her own brain roiled with possibilities. Perhaps simply having her grandfather's portrait was adding to Annabelle's power. Perhaps the McMartins had a spy—someone like Mrs. Nivens or the painted Horatio—passing them news of what went on inside the old stone house. Or perhaps something else was happening . . . Something that no one would expect or recognize until it was too late.

Olive glanced up at her new neighbors. *What if . . . ?* she wondered. But Rutherford trusted them. Mrs. Dewey trusted them. And Delora had just described Olive's parents, right down to the ink on Mr. Dunwoody's sleeve. Clearly she had been telling the truth.

Another gust of wind struck the house. The walls groaned softly. A spattering of dead leaves clicked against the front door.

"We will commence a thorough search of the area first thing tomorrow morning," Doctor Widdecombe said, breaking the silence. "But, for now, some of us need our sleep." He gave Olive an authoritative nod. "Under the circumstances, I think the wisest course of action would be for Olive to leave this house. Delora and I will remain here, keeping watch, and Olive can stay with Mrs. Dewey. Can't she, Lydia?"

"Of course." Mrs. Dewey squeezed Olive's shoulder. "She can stay with us just as long as she likes."

With her body wedged tight against Mrs. Dewey's squishy side, Olive's mind sprang up and raced through the rooms of the old stone house. It climbed up and down staircases and peered through darkened doorways. It counted the treasures that waited everywhere: the painted entrances to Elsewhere, the odd antiques, the hidden attic, the secret tunnel beneath the basement. The strange old house itself.

The cats would never abandon this place. Not if it stood here for centuries to come. And the people of Elsewhere, the always-painted and the once-alive, wouldn't leave it either. They *couldn't* leave.

They needed her.

"No," said Olive.

Doctor Widdecombe's eyebrows went up. "What was that, Olive?"

"No," said Olive, more clearly. "I'm not leaving."

"Olive . . ." Delora's worried eyes came to rest somewhere in the vicinity of Olive's hairline. "I can sense that trouble will return." Her gaze floated from Olive's head toward the ceiling. "Yes," she whispered. "Grave danger is coming to this place."

"It was already here," said Olive.

Doctor Widdecombe's expression was gentle. "Olive, my dear, you must realize that three adults—one a green witch, one a gifted messenger, and one a world-renowned expert on dark magic—may be better able to handle this situation."

Walter cleared his throat.

"Excuse me, Walter," said Doctor Widdecombe. "*Four* adults."

"No," said Olive. The vehemence in her voice made everyone give a little jump, including Olive herself. "This is my house, and I won't leave it."

"Child—" Delora began, but Mrs. Dewey cut her off.

"Olive has had enough trouble for one night," she said. "I think she should get to do whatever would make her most comfortable."

"Then perhaps she will permit us to remain in the house with her." Doctor Widdecombe looked down at Olive with genuine worry in his eyes. "She cannot stay here *alone*."

"I'm not alone," said Olive. "I have the cats. And Morton."

"Let me stay," Walter spoke up. "I'll stand guard on the porch. And—mmm—I'll alert everyone if anything happens." He shoved his sleeves to the top of his spindly arms. The sleeves slid straight back down. "I mean, if I'm no good with magic, I can at least provide the muscle."

There was a snort. Everyone turned to look at Doctor Widdecombe, who pulled a handkerchief from his pocket and pretended to blow his nose.

"What do you think, Olive?" asked Mrs. Dewey. "Would that be all right with you? Or would you like me and Rutherford to stay too?"

Olive glanced around at the people encircling her like a sympathetic cage. She didn't want anyone else taking charge of things—no matter who that *anyone else* was. This was *her* house. And what she wanted now was to be alone inside of it, to begin to make sense of everything that had happened without any other voices getting in the way.

"Just Walter can stay," she said. "And just on the porch."

Delora wavered at the foot of the staircase, her pale hands folded over her chest. "I fear for you, Olive," she whispered, staring into the air above Olive's head again. "This place will only bring you harm."

Doctor Widdecombe took Delora gently by the arm. Delora fell silent.

"First thing tomorrow," Doctor Widdecombe said, in a cheerier voice, "we'll complete a search of the area, and then we will return to safeguard the house—if we haven't already found your parents, that is," he added. His eyes flicked once more to the darkness at the other end of the hallway. "Walter will make a perfectly adequate bodyguard, I'm sure. And now, once again, we shall bid you all good night."

With a final seam-straining bow, he guided Delora out the front door.

Walter ducked his head and hunched his shoulders. To Olive, he looked more than ever like a long-legged water bird—but now the bird was watching the water for predators. Or prey. "Mmm . . . I'll be on the porch," he said, in his deep voice. "If you need me." Then he stepped through the door and closed it soundly behind him.

Mrs. Dewey gave Olive a final, sweet-scented hug before getting up to put on her coat. "If you change your mind, just let us know."

Rutherford leaned over the banister. "From what I could hear of their thoughts, both Doctor Widdecombe and Delora were quite certain that you ought to leave the house," he said into Olive's ear. "They may be right about something dangerous approaching."

"I'll be careful," Olive murmured back. "But I'm not leaving."

Rutherford watched Olive for a moment, his eyes

wide and solemn behind their smudged lenses. Then he gave a little nod and backed away.

From her spot on the bottom step, Olive listened to Rutherford and Mrs. Dewey telling Walter good night, and to their footsteps thumping across the porch and down the steps before dwindling away into the whispering darkness.

Finally, the house was still.

Several seconds passed before Olive heard the rustle of fabric. Morton scooted down the stairs to Olive's step. He pulled back his ghostly hood. Without saying a word, he wrapped one skinny arm around her back, and then, so softly she wasn't sure she felt it at all, he began to pat her on one shoulder. And that was how they sat, not speaking, until Olive was ready to stand up again.

* * * * *

Everyone stayed in Olive's room that night. The reading lamp formed a glowing barricade around the bed where Olive lay, still dressed in her jabberwocky sweat suit. Hershel, her worn brown bear, sagged comfortingly against her chest. The three cats positioned themselves around her, Leopold at her feet, Horatio at her side, and Harvey near her head. Morton sprawled on the floor, just beyond the border of the light. Annabelle's filigreed locket, which had once held her grandfather's portrait, glimmered on Olive's vanity like a poisonous reminder. Olive could almost see Aldous's portrait slithering out of it, swelling to fill the house with darkness. With a deep breath, she pulled her eyes away.

Olive set her father's glasses very carefully on the bedside table, so she would know just where they were when he came back. And he *would* come back, she told herself. Their lenses looked cold and empty in the yellow light.

"Nothing else appears to have been taken," said Horatio, his sharp eyes fixed on Olive's face. "The grimoire is still safely hidden. The paintings and other furnishings are all where they belong."

"The tunnel is untouched," said Leopold.

"The attic is undisturbed as well," added Harvey, wriggling out of his robe and unfastening the pincushion that had formed the Hunchcat's hump.

Olive nodded. She knew she should feel relieved by this news, but she didn't. There wasn't room left inside her to feel anything at all.

"Tomorrow we will continue our search. Against us, with all of our allies on Linden Street, Annabelle will not stand a chance." Horatio's tail flicked over Olive's arm, almost like a soothing hand. "We will find your parents, Olive."

Olive looked down at Morton. He had curled up in a small white ball in the shadows, with his face tilted up toward hers. He didn't speak, but Olive knew what he must be thinking. The McMartins had taken *his* parents too, and they still hadn't been found.

They might never be found.

Quiet settled throughout the room like raindrops filling an empty cup. Outside, beyond the window, the twigs of the leafless ash tree clattered softly. Olive was sure she wouldn't be able to fall asleep, but her eyelids insisted on sliding shut, and she felt too hollow and heavy to pull them back up. There was a last whispering rush of wind, and then even the darkness disappeared.

9

"OLIVE," CALLED HER mother's voice.

The voice was soft and far away, floating toward Olive's ears through a wall of wispy gray clouds. A hand tapped lightly at her door. "Olive, it's time to get up," her mother called again. "You're already running thirteen point five minutes late for the school bus . . ."

Olive's eyes slid open.

Her bedroom was lit by gray morning light. A set of wire wings, two rumpled gloves, and a pair of painted goggles lay in a pile on the floor beyond the edge of her bed.

Olive frowned down at the goggles. That's right—this was the day after Halloween. That meant that this was Sunday. And *Sunday* meant that she didn't have to go to school. She didn't have to go *anywhere*. She didn't have a thing to do but pour her haul of candy onto her bedspread and sort the treats into Most Delicious, Semi-Tasty, and Still Better Than Pickled Beets piles. Smiling to herself, Olive snuggled back into her pillows.

The branches of the ash tree tapped gently at the windowpane. *That's* what she had heard when she thought someone was knocking at her door. And her mother hadn't been calling for her to get up, because her mother was—

Her mother was . . .

Olive sat up.

The hollowness of the house seemed to widen around her. She could feel the stillness on every side, filling the rooms and hallways in place of the burbling coffeepot and clicking computer keys. Her heartbeat echoed in the emptiness.

On the pillow beside her, a damp orange cat began to stir.

"I hope we did not wake you," said Horatio, running a paw over his whiskers. "You needed a good night's sleep as much as I needed a bath."

Olive looked blearily around. Morton's ghost costume lay crumpled on the rug. Leopold's sash hung neatly over the back of the vanity chair. "Where is everyone?" she asked.

"Harvey took Morton home some time ago. The morning light was making him uncomfortable. Leopold is surveying the grounds."

"Oh." Olive pulled her knees to her chest, hugging herself tight. "Should you be guarding your territory too?"

"I've been guarding *you*," Horatio answered. He stopped brushing his whiskers, and his penetrating green eyes settled on Olive's face. "You are not alone here, Olive."

Olive tried to give Horatio a smile, but the best she could manage was a twitchy grimace. "Actually, I'd *like* to be alone for a few minutes," she said. "I need to change my clothes."

Once the cat had padded into the hallway, Olive hauled her legs out of bed and trudged across the room to her dresser. Her body felt as though it had been scooped out and refilled with wet sand. She could barely manage to yank a sweater over her head and wriggle into a pair of jeans.

Once she was dressed, Olive shuffled out into the hall. Each creak of the floorboards seemed to thunder through the house. Sounds that disappeared on an ordinary day—the buzz of the refrigerator, the low breath of the furnace huffing from far below—hung in the air, startling and strange. Even the paintings along the staircase seemed to have noticed the change in the house. A dark glint shifted over their surfaces as Olive passed by, like multiplied shadows gliding after her.

By the time she reached the foot of the staircase, Olive felt too heavy to take another step. She gazed down at the rug, still twisted to one side, and the candy scattered across the floor like colorfully wrapped hailstones.

A board creaked on the front porch. Olive glanced up as Walter's lanky silhouette paced across the windows. Leopold was out there somewhere, patrolling the lawn. Next door, a pair of odd but kindly witches was waiting to help her, and in the house one door beyond that, a boy and his grandmother were probably just waking up and beginning to collect the ingredients for a new set of spells.

She *wasn't* alone.

Olive took a deep breath.

Then she knelt down and began to gather the candy back into its bowl, counting the pieces out loud to herself as she went.

When she'd dropped in the last one (there were eighty-four pieces, she was almost sure), Olive pushed herself back to her feet. She looked around the empty hallway. She'd left the hall lights burning all night long, but in the morning sun, they looked watery and faint, like cellophane wrappers with nothing left inside. She switched them off, watching the paintings on the walls dim from glinting sheets of color into something darker, and a thought struck her so suddenly that it almost knocked her back to the floor.

What if—somehow—Annabelle had been able to trap Olive's parents Elsewhere? What if they were stuck there right now, watching Olive drift through the empty rooms while their bodies turned slowly into paint?

"Horatio!" Olive screamed.

The cat appeared at the head of the stairs. "What?" he asked. "What did you find?"

Olive darted to the bottom step. "Horatio—the grimoire is safe, isn't it?"

"It remains in the very spot where I hid it myself."

Olive clutched the front of her shirt. "And I've still got the spectacles—but what if Annabelle found some other way to put my parents Elsewhere?" She wrapped both hands around the banister, clutching it so hard her wrists ached. "Wouldn't that be the worst thing she could do? Trapping them right here, in their own house, where we wouldn't even think to look for them?"

"Olive, it is extremely unlikely that Annabelle could have—"

"Stop!" Olive shouted. "You sound like Rutherford! Please, Horatio, I have to make sure. It might already be too late!"

Horatio's whiskers twitched. "Very well. I'll tell Leopold to search the paintings on the main floor and Harvey to examine each canvas in the attic. You and I will search upstairs."

"Yes!" Olive exclaimed, scrambling back up the staircase as Horatio flew down. "And please hurry!"

Olive tore to the left, toward her parents' end of the hallway. In the small white room on the right, which contained nothing but stacks of unpacked boxes, Olive shoved the spectacles onto her face. The room's only painting depicted a grumpy-looking bird on a fencepost. As Olive plunged through its frame, the bird took off, squeaking and squawking into the sky. The rest of the painting was uninhabited. A few stalks of grass shivered against the fence, and the green field and blue sky loomed around her as solidly as walls.

"Mom!" Olive called. "Dad!" But even the grumpy bird had stopped squawking.

In her parents' bedroom, Olive swallowed a sob at the familiar sights and smells: her mother's chalk-dusted brown cardigan hanging over the back of a chair, the minty scent of her father's aftershave, and the big white bed, with its perfectly symmetrical arrangement of pillows. But there wasn't time to sprawl on the bed and cry, messing up all of its right angles.

Olive dashed across the room, hanging on tight to the bottom of the picture frame as she pushed her head into the painting of an old-fashioned sailing ship. A blast of salty ocean wind whished through her hair. Below her, the purplish waves rippled and roared.

"Dad! Mom!" she shouted over the sound. "Are you here?"

There was no answer.

Olive waited, watching the ship rock slowly back and forth, never getting closer to its port. Then she pulled herself back through the jelly-ish surface and dropped to the bedroom floor.

In the room's other painting, a tall, slender man sat reading a book in a gazebo, surrounded by a lush green garden. He bolted to his feet, dropping his book and catching it awkwardly again as Olive clambered through the frame.

"Holy cats!" said the man. "You can climb *in* here?"

Olive stumbled to her feet. There was no time to answer questions. And there certainly was no time to be shy. Cautious, maybe—but not shy. Keeping her back near the frame, she demanded, "Have you seen my parents?"

The lanky man tucked the book under one arm. "Your parents?" he repeated. "I think so. Yes. Well, yes and no."

Olive's heart shot up like a rocket, then took a rapid nosedive. "What?"

"Yes," said the lanky man. "I've seen 'em. They sleep

right out there, don't they?" The man pointed through the frame, at the Dunwoodys' deserted bedroom. "But last night, they didn't."

"Oh," said Olive. "But they haven't come *in here,* have they?"

"No," said the man. "No sirree. I've been alone in here for"—his eyes traveled around the painted glade, as if they were looking for a clue—"oh, I don't know," he finished, when they didn't find one. "It's been a long time."

Olive nodded, wheeling back toward the frame. "Thank you," she called over her shoulder.

"Wait!" The man darted forward, following her along the cobblestone path. "Do you have to leave again so soon?" He held out one long-fingered hand. "I'm Robert. Roberto the Magnificent, that is. Maybe you've heard of me?"

"No," said Olive, with a quick shake of the man's hand. The man's *warm* hand. This man had once been alive. Placing her fingers on the bottom of the picture frame, she gave his narrow, eager face a closer look.

"How about Binkle and Rudd's World-Wandering Carnival?"

"No," said Olive again. "Sorry."

"I was the main attraction." The lanky man pointed at his chest. "Traveling magician. Watch." The man made a little explosive gesture, and a bouquet of paper roses popped out of his sleeve. "For you, little lady," he announced. The roses shot back up his sleeve before he could grab them.

"My tricks don't work too well in here." The man sighed. "And that's all they were. *Tricks.* I told the old man, I said, 'Look, I'm a sleight-of-hand artist. A carnival performer.' But he said I should be grateful he was just confining me, not destroying me like he'd done to the others."

Olive stared up into the magician's face. "Was this 'old man' really tall and bony, with deep eyes and—"

"And a voice that sounds like he eats gravel for breakfast?" The magician nodded intently. "That's him."

"I know who he is," said Olive. "He and—" A lump of something hard and icy formed at the back of her throat. "He and his granddaughter have taken my parents." She whirled back toward the frame. "I'm sorry," she called over her shoulder. "I need to keep looking."

"Do you really have to go?" The man transferred his little book—*Cleverton's Completely Confounding Card Tricks!* read the cover—from under one arm to the other, rooting in his jacket pockets. "I think I had a pack of cards in here . . ."

"I'm sorry," said Olive again, with one leg already through the frame. "But I'll come back and visit sometime."

When Olive landed on her parents' bedroom floor

and glanced back up at the canvas, Roberto the Magnificent was walking slowly back toward the gazebo, his shoulders slumped and his head bowed.

Olive felt a little tug of guilt. But she had to get back to the search. There was no time to spare. She raced into the hallway. A few steps ahead of her, Horatio's furry orange form dove through the frame around the moonlit forest and landed on the faded carpet. He looked up at Olive. "No sign of them in the forest," he reported. "Morton's neighbors haven't seen them either, and Morton's had them searching every house on the street."

"Would you check Annabelle's empty portrait?" Olive asked. "I'll take the paintings in the blue room."

With a nod, Horatio shot off like a fuzzy orange arrow, and Olive pounded along the hall to the blue bedroom, plunging into the painting of the grand ball.

"Olive!" shouted the dancers.

"Olive!" shouted the musicians in the orchestra.

"Olive!" shouted the conductor, still waving his baton even though the music had stopped. "Will you join us for a waltz?"

"I can't," panted Olive. "I'm looking for someone. You haven't seen any *new* people in here, have you?"

The conductor blinked at Olive. "Is this a trick question?"

"I mean my mom and dad. I thought they might be

here, hidden in the crowd." Olive wove through the pairs of dancers. "Mom! Dad!"

"Mom!" shouted some of the dancers. "Dad!" shouted the others. Soon everybody in the painted ballroom was shouting "Mom! Dad! Mom! Dad!" but nobody was answering.

"Thank you," Olive called, rushing back toward the frame, leaving the musicians happily twanging and plucking to the rhythm of their new chant.

The porter in the painted castle was delighted to see Olive too.

"Back for another tour?" he boomed as Olive skidded across the mossy drawbridge.

"I'm looking for my parents," Olive puffed. "Have you seen them?"

The porter glanced around. "I know every inch of this castle," he said, raising his lantern so that its beams fell over the dark stone floors and crumbling walls. High above, painted stars flecked the deep blue sky. "And I can tell you this: Your parents are not here."

Olive met Horatio in the doorway of the blue bedroom.

"No luck," said the cat.

"Me neither," said Olive sadly. She pointed to the painting of a bowl of odd fruits hanging on the wall between two bedroom doors. "I suppose we'd better check in there."

Horatio looked slightly startled. "I don't think we'll find your parents inside a bowl of fruit, Olive."

"But we might find something *else*," Olive argued. "Let's look, just to be sure."

Thanks to Ms. Teedlebaum's art class, Olive knew that this kind of painting was called a still life. Olive's class had painted still lifes of their own, using whatever objects they could extract from the clutter in Ms. Teedlebaum's classroom, which had made for some very strange compositions. Olive's own still life had included a rubber chicken, a pack of gum, and a toilet plunger. Aldous McMartin's still life was far more beautiful, but no less strange. Inside the painting's dark-walled room, Olive stared down into the bowl of fruit. Horatio perched on the table, following her movements with sharp green eyes.

"My parents aren't here, obviously," said Olive. "But maybe there's a clue at the bottom of this bowl—a hidden key or a map or something." She grabbed the wide silver dish and spilled the fruits across the table, but there was nothing hidden underneath. The moment she turned the bowl upright, the fruits flew back to their usual positions inside it. Olive bent lower, squinting at the bowl's contents.

The painted bowl was filled with something that looked like aquamarine grapes, and pink-peeled citrus fruits, and a yellowish object that had a long, looping vine and was shaped like a teardrop. Olive sniffed at one cylindrical orange fruit. It smelled fruity—in the way that a candy store smells fruity, as though a bunch of strong, separate flavors had been poured together to concoct something new.

"Maybe these are magical," she said thoughtfully, with the fruit still smooshed against her nose. "Maybe if I take a bite, I'll shrink, or see things, or fly, or something."

"Or *something*, yes," said Horatio warningly. "Get poisoned, or something. Throw up all over this table, or something."

"I'm going to try it," said Olive, turning away from Horatio's frown. She took a tiny bite.

The fruit was crunchy, and tasted like an unripe pear soaked in orange juice. Before Olive had time to chew it, her mouth was empty. The fruit in her hand was whole once again, the little indents left by her teeth rapidly mending and disappearing.

"How do you feel?" asked Horatio, watching her closely.

"Just the same," said Olive softly, putting the fruit back into the bowl.

"Come along." Horatio's voice was milder now. "We have one more painting to check."

At the end of the hall, just outside the pink bedroom, a painting of a Scottish hillside hung in a shadowy patch of the wall. Olive shuddered, gazing through the frame at the rippling bracken, the swooping birds, the small stone church perched high on the hill. In the foreground, nearly covered by heather and gorse, an oily smudge marked the spot where Olive had encountered a younger, painted version of Aldous McMartin and—with Rutherford's help, and a few well-aimed squirts of paint thinner—dissolved him into nothing.

"I will examine the forest and the cottage," said Horatio, seeing Olive's hesitation. "You can check the hilltop; it's much lighter up there. He's *gone,* Olive," the cat added as Olive adjusted the spectacles with shaky fingers. "We will be safe."

"I know," Olive whispered. "It's just . . . I know."

The bracken crackled softly under her shoes as she landed inside the painting. Leaping in after her, Horatio cut a path toward the yellow-leafed forest, the orange tips of his ears dwindling quickly out of sight amid the brush. Olive took a deep breath. Giving the smudged spot a wide berth, she trotted up the hillside.

The church's wooden doors opened with a creak. Inside, dusty daylight streamed through the high windows and burnished the wood of the empty pews. "Dad?" Olive's voice rang against the walls. "Mom?" Even without waiting for an answer, she could tell that she was the only one there.

Olive stepped back out through the doors, into

the small cemetery that clustered close to the church. Its gravestones were weathered and soft, brushed by the butter-pale sun. These were nothing like the cold, broken stones built into the walls of the basement. Olive wound between the ancient plots, running her fingers over the slightly warm stones. She paused beside a pair of angular headstones that leaned together in a friendly way, their faces overgrown by painted ferns and wildflowers. Olive brushed her fingers over the edge of one stone. Strange—this stone felt *wrong*, somehow. It felt smoother and sharper than the others, which were as pocked and porous as English muffins. This stone felt *newer*. Mildly curious, Olive crouched down and brushed the fluttering ferns aside.

An icy wind surged through her body. It numbed her heart, freezing her lungs and pummeling her stomach. The ferns pulled themselves swiftly back into their places, but Olive had had plenty of time to read the two simple words carved beneath.

Mother, said one. *Father,* said the other.

"HORATIO!" OLIVE SCREAMED. "Horatio!" Her
voice blew away over the rippling hillside.

An orange streak barreled up from the valley below.
"Olive!" Horatio leaped over the crest of the hill,
racing toward her through the graveyard. "Are you all
right?"

Olive pointed at the headstones, her arm trembling.
"These aren't—" The question stuck in her dry mouth.
"These aren't—?"

"*No*, Olive," said Horatio firmly. "Those are not
your mother and father. I promise you."

Olive pressed her hands hard against her aching
chest, feeling slightly silly. "I just—I couldn't remember if these two stones had been here before, and they
looked different from the others . . ."

"They *are* different," said Horatio. He sat down

beside Olive, facing the overgrown headstones. "Annabelle McMartin brought them here herself, long after this painting was completed."

"Why?" Olive asked. Her heart gave another tightening clench. "Oh no. She—you mean—these aren't *Morton's* mother and father, are they?"

"No," Horatio answered. "They are Annabelle's."

Olive's heart began to beat again. "Annabelle's?"

"Albert McMartin—Aldous's only son—had no talent for magic. Or anything else, for that matter. He was kind, and lazy, and stupid." Horatio looked away from the graves, his eyes flickering over the sunny hillside. "But he was not so stupid that he couldn't see the evil in his own father. And after years of watching neighbors disappear, Albert got off his lazy backside and took action." Horatio's voice grew softer, even though there was no one around to hear. "One night, when Aldous McMartin was away, Albert built a huge fire in the library fireplace and burned all of Aldous's self-portraits, one after another. Then he fled the house with his wife and daughter. But Annabelle was already a young woman—a stubborn, cruel young woman—and she worshipped her grandfather. She sent him a message revealing everything that her father had done. Naturally, Aldous was furious. He hauled them all back to this house, called his son a traitor, accused him of trying to destroy the family, and . . ."

Horatio hesitated. "That was that," he concluded quietly. "After Aldous disposed of Albert and his wife, he interred them here, inside Elsewhere, where no outsiders could ever find them." Horatio's eyes darted back to the graves. "Much later, after Aldous himself had died, Annabelle had the headstones carved and placed them here."

"She did?" Olive wavered, looking down at the simple stones. "Why?"

"Annabelle McMartin was not a good person, Olive," said Horatio. "But she wasn't the monster that Aldous had hoped to raise. And Aldous himself may be to blame for that."

Olive watched the wildflowers fluttering over the carved names. "I can't believe Aldous could kill his own son," she said. "I mean—didn't Albert's *mother* mind?"

Horatio stiffened slightly. "By that time, Aldous's wife was long gone." The cat cocked one furry eyebrow. "And you should not underestimate Aldous's pride. He believed that his family tree bore the greatest magicians who had ever lived, that each generation would grow more powerful, more intelligent, more ruthless—and then his own son turned out to be a failure. Annabelle McMartin was his last hope. Now that even she is gone . . . in a human sense . . . the family has no heir."

Olive nodded down at the quiet graves. "And that's just what the real Ms. McMartin wanted. For the family to fade away."

"But that is not what this *house* wants." Horatio's eyes glittered up at Olive. "You've made it clear that you won't join their side—at least, not without a fight. And you don't have any magical talent *at all*."

Olive's shoulders sagged. "Oh."

"Don't be disappointed," Horatio snapped. "That is a good thing, I assure you. It may well have saved your life already." He turned back toward the graves. "But I believe . . . and I fear . . . that the McMartins are seeking someone to train. Someone to take on this house. Someone with gifts that *you* do not possess, and without the conscience that you *do*. And they will need to find him before their power is worn away completely."

For a moment, they stood side by side as the wind rustled over the heather and one blackbird wheeled in the pale, painted sky.

"You know what I think?" said Olive as they headed back down through the bracken on the hill. "I think I'm *never* going to come into this painting again."

"I can't say that I blame you," said Horatio.

"I mean, if I had known that there were actual—"

Olive stopped. Far below them, where the picture frame hung in midair, a large black cat had just zoomed into the painting like something launched from a giant's slingshot.

"Information to report, miss!" Leopold shouted from the foot of the hill. "There were witnesses to the invasion! Come with me!"

Olive and Horatio broke into a run.

Downstairs, the kitchen was eerily still. Sunday mornings in the old stone house usually meant stacks of Mr. Dunwoody's pancakes (he claimed to have discovered the ideal ratio of butter to maple syrup), fresh orange juice for Olive, and several pots of coffee for Mr. and Mrs. Dunwoody, which would keep the coffeepot puffing and steaming away until afternoon.

But not today.

No pancakes sizzled softly on the stove. No coffee-scented mathematicians bustled back and forth between the worn stone counters. Today, the room felt almost hungrily empty, like a cupboard with nothing on its shelves.

Olive and Horatio followed Leopold to the corner, near the painting of three stonemasons at work on a wall.

Leopold cleared his throat. "If you don't object, miss, I shall let you enter on your own. There was a bit of unpleasantness during my own sojourn, and I was forced to depart without gathering the necessary information."

"I understand," said Olive. "I'll be right back."

Ducking her head and squeezing her shoulders to her ears, Olive wedged herself through the painting's small frame. Before her feet had hit the ground, a massive, furry missile had knocked her backward into the grass. Olive blinked up at the painted sky as a slobbering brown dog bounced around her, snuffling at her ears and licking her chin.

"Off, Baltus. Get *off*," Olive muttered.

"Sorry about that, Miss Olive," said one of the three stonemasons at work on the never-finished wall. "He's still pretty excited about our visit from that cat."

"I'll bet," said Olive, managing to roll out from under Baltus's kisses.

"You're not hurt?" the second mason asked, leaning over the wall for a closer look and knocking a stone out of its place. It floated back to its spot like a granite soap bubble.

"I'm fine," said Olive, hurrying toward the wall. Baltus trotted beside her. "Leopold said that you saw something last night."

"Indeed we did." The first mason removed his cap to scratch his head. He glanced at the other two for support. Then he looked at Olive out of the corner of his eyes, as though she'd just caught him composing a love poem. ". . . Monsters," he mumbled.

"*Monsters?*" Olive echoed.

"There were monsters." He pointed to the frame. "Out there."

"There were monsters in the kitchen?" Olive pictured Dracula squeezing a bag of oranges while Swamp Thing flipped a pancake. "What kind of monsters?"

"Werewolves," said the third mason. "I'm quite sure they were werewolves."

"And there was a mummy," the second mason put in.

"How many monsters were there?" asked Olive as Baltus shoved his nose under her wrist and began licking her fingers.

"Three," said the second mason, his eyes wide.

"Four," the third mason argued.

"Three or four, I think," said the first mason. His voice was hushed and nervous. "They all walked upright, even the werewolves. Baltus was barking to beat the band." He glanced at Baltus, who was coating Olive's arm with a gradually disappearing sheet of slobber. He bent down and grasped a stick. "Fetch, boy!" he shouted, hurling the stick into the distance.

Baltus took off like a furry freight train. The stick reappeared in its spot beside the wall.

"Poor fellow never catches it," said the mason, shaking his head at Baltus's dwindling backside.

Olive looked around at the nervous men. Of course they were nervous; they'd just seen three (or four) monsters walk past their picture frame. Olive knew how it felt to see something inhuman lurch out of the corner of your eye, to feel it staring back at you from the sunken pits in a warped, rubbery face . . .

"Wait," she said. "Do you think that the monsters could have been people? People in masks and costumes?"

The masons looked at one another.

"I suppose they *could* have been . . ." said the first.

"When they came into the kitchen, what did they do?" Olive asked urgently.

"They were struggling with something," said the third mason. "Some of them were pushing and pulling at the others. And then they all went out through the back door."

Olive bit the inside of her cheek while these facts plummeted into place. Of course. How clever . . . and how *convenient*. If Annabelle had sneaked into the house in a Halloween costume, she would have been welcomed by her smiling victims. Then she could have disguised Mr. and Mrs. Dunwoody in costumes too, and smuggled them back out of the place right under the neighbors' nosy noses. It was just like Olive's own plan for Morton.

In Olive's chest, a drum began to pound.

"Thank you!" she shouted, wheeling toward the frame.

"Come and see us anytime!" the masons called after her. "We'll keep an eye out for you!"

Olive hit the kitchen tiles with a smack. "They saw

three or four creatures that looked like monsters," she panted, crouching down between the waiting cats. "But they might have been people in costumes. And two of those people could have been my parents!"

"Clever," said Horatio.

"An artful maneuver," added Leopold.

"The question is: Was Annabelle acting alone, or—"

A knock from the front door echoed down the hallway. A split second later, a splotchily colored cat came streaking around the kitchen corner.

"Agent 1-800, reporting," Harvey announced in a faintly British accent, bumping his way through their huddle and coming nose to nose with Olive. "Our fellow agents have returned. At this point, I suggest we abandon surveillance in favor of intelligence-gathering, until we are all as intelligent as we can be. Agreed?"

"Agreed," said Leopold. Olive nodded. Horatio sighed.

Harvey spoke into the imaginary transistor watch on his left front paw. "Agent 1-800 to headquarters," he muttered. "Do you read? Have you read any good books lately?"

"Who do you think you are talking to, Harvey?" asked Horatio. "Do you have an extra ear growing between your toes?"

"Agent Orange!" Harvey's eyes widened, as though

he were recognizing Horatio for the first time. "You received my signal. Our ally agents await our appearance at the rendezvous point."

"You mean, someone's at the door?" Olive asked.

Harvey seemed to struggle with himself. Then, in his smallest, sulkiest voice, he muttered, ". . . Yes."

Olive peeped through the front windows. Rutherford, Mrs. Dewey, Walter, Delora, and Doctor Widdecombe were clustered on the porch. After tucking the spectacles safely under her collar, Olive flung the door open.

"Someone saw what happened last night! Someone Elsewhere!" she said, before anyone else could say *Good morning,* or *Hello, Olive,* or *Why are your pants covered with dog slobber?* "I think Annabelle—and maybe someone *else*—got inside of the house in Halloween costumes, and then took my parents out the back door, in disguise!"

"Ah," said Doctor Widdecombe, tossing his scarf onto the coatrack. "Then we can be certain that they were indeed removed from the house. An important elimination."

"Yet we found no sign of them anywhere in the neighborhood," said Delora, unwrapping a long black velvet cloak to reveal a long black velvet dress beneath. "But I foresaw that our search would not be a simple one."

"Well—if we know they're not in the house, shouldn't we get back out *there* again?" Olive asked, grabbing her jacket from the rack and shoving one arm into the wrong sleeve. "Where have you already looked? Maybe we—"

"Olive," Doctor Widdecombe interrupted, "we must conduct a search of the house itself before we go any farther."

Olive stuffed the proper arm into the sleeve and wriggled the other one free. "But the cats and I already checked the house," she said, moving toward the open door. "They aren't here."

"It's not only your parents we must look for," said Delora.

"Before we can understand Annabelle's plans, we must know just what it is that she prizes—what motivates her, what gives her power, what draws her back to this house," Doctor Widdecombe explained.

"But—"

"Olive." Doctor Widdecombe lowered his voice. He stepped toward her, his hands clasped humbly against his belly. "You've seen how powerful Delora's gifts are . . ."

A gust of wind swirled through the open door. Olive twisted the doorknob in her hand, recalling the feeling of relief that had swirled through her in the same way when Delora promised that the Dunwoodys were alive.

"And I assure you, I know a bit about magic myself," Doctor Widdecombe went on, giving Olive a twinkly little smile and wink. "Letting us examine this house will be anything but a waste of time."

Olive took a breath. She glanced around at the faces of her guests all gathered in the entrance, watching her, and felt like one smallish malamute trying to pull a house-sized sled.

"All right," she said, forcing her impatience down. "We can search the house first."

Doctor Widdecombe beamed.

Olive pushed the heavy front door shut.

"Olive dear," said Mrs. Dewey brightly, "would you mind if I used your kitchen?" She held up a shopping bag full of things that couldn't have been bought in any store for a thousand miles. "We have some indoor charms to concoct, and my Locksleaf needs to simmer for another ten minutes, at least."

Olive nodded. The adults headed down the hall toward the kitchen, Mrs. Dewey tip-tapping in her little high heels, Doctor Widdecombe strolling after her, and Delora drifting behind them both like black velvet smoke.

"Can I help?" Walter offered. "I could—"

"No, Walter," said Delora over one shoulder. "We've no need of you."

Walter's shoulders sagged.

Harvey bumped against Olive's shin. "Reconnaissance mission under way," he muttered from the corner of his mouth. "Agent 1-800 is on the move." With a sharp nod, he slunk after the disappearing guests.

Olive, Rutherford, and Walter stood together in the entryway. Even without his ghoul costume, there was something strangely out of scale about Walter. Maybe it was that too-deep voice coming from his skinny neck. Maybe it was the long, bony arms that seemed to reach almost to his knees. Maybe it was the way he towered a full head and shoulders over his aunt and uncle, while they still treated him like a child. None of it made Olive feel any more comfortable around him.

Olive kept her arms folded tight across her chest. Horatio and Leopold flanked her like fuzzy gargoyles. Walter shifted on his feet, casting occasional sad looks along the hall toward the kitchen. Only Rutherford seemed at ease.

"Tell me, Walter," he began brightly, "what was it like to grow up with a world-renowned magical authority like Doctor Widdecombe in your family?"

"Mmm," said Walter. "Um . . . He only married my aunt Delora a couple of years ago." Walter's bony shoulders began to rise. "And she's always traveled a lot, so I didn't see much of either of them until my mother died and Delora took me in. She calls me her apprentice, but it's not really—*I'm* not really—I'm not like her." Walter's shoulders had risen to his ears at this point. Olive wondered if they would keep rising until they came together above Walter's head. "I'm grateful for everything Doctor Widdecombe—I mean Doctor Uncle—I mean Uncle Byron has done for me," Walter went on. "I'd like to show him—show *both* of them— that I *do* have promise. That teaching me wouldn't be a waste. But I'd need to surprise them, or do something really important, or . . ." Walter trailed off. The bony shoulders shrugged. "It's hard to impress somebody who's already the best at everything you try."

Olive felt a pang of recognition. She felt that very same feeling every time she picked up a calculator to check her math homework, and one of her parents gave the answer faster than Olive could press the equals button. She looked up at Walter, chewing on her lower lip and thinking that he'd probably just said more words in a row than he'd said in all their other conversations put together.

"Well," announced Mrs. Dewey from the kitchen door, "the leaves are simmering. I'll make us all some tea in a bit." She clicked back down the hallway, followed by Doctor Widdecombe, with Delora on his arm. Harvey skulked behind them like a splotchy shadow. "Olive, have you eaten today?" Mrs. Dewey continued. "Perhaps I'll make some lunch as well."

"Lunch would be delightful," said Doctor Widdecombe before Olive could answer. "But first, we will whet our appetites with a thorough search." He gestured toward the library doors. "Shall we begin?"

"The three of us will guard what ought *not* to be discovered," Horatio murmured to Olive as the others headed toward the library. "And Olive," he added, while Harvey zoomed up the staircase and Leopold marched toward the basement door, "give away as little as is necessary. Even to our allies. Each time a secret is shared, it grows less safe." With a last sharp look at Olive, he turned to follow Harvey up the stairs.

A creak echoed through the hallway. Doctor Widdecombe had thrown open the library's double doors. By the time Olive caught up with them, Doctor Widdecombe had led everyone inside. Light from the tall windows glazed the fireplace's painted tiles. Oriental rugs stretched across the floor, their patterns paling in the sun. Shelves bearing thousands of books towered to the ceilings, the gilt and leather of their spines glimmering in the grayish daylight.

Delora gave a delicate gasp.

"Wow," Walter murmured.

Rutherford and Mrs. Dewey, who had seen this room before, kept quiet.

"What a trove!" Doctor Widdecombe exclaimed, striding to the center of the room. "There must be thousands of volumes here!"

Olive's stomach gave a twist. Once, her father had

helped her estimate the total number of books in the library, but she couldn't remember the answer anymore—and these thousands of books seemed small and unimportant now anyway. She hovered beside her mother's desk, tapping her fingers impatiently on its surface.

"Wow," said Walter again, tilting his head sideways to read a row of spines. "Are they all about magic?"

"No," said Olive quickly. "None of them are. I've looked."

"How very odd," said Doctor Widdecombe. "Perhaps the McMartins hid their grimoires and recipes and bestiaries in a more unexpected location, for safekeeping."

Olive scuffed her toes along a curlicue in the faded rug. "Maybe." She glanced up, meeting Rutherford's eyes. He stared back at her for a moment, frowning slightly. *Please don't tell them,* she thought. *Please don't tell them.* Still frowning, Rutherford gave a little nod.

"And this must be another of Aldous's artworks," Doctor Widdecombe went on, approaching the huge painting of several white-gowned girls dancing in a meadow. He gazed up at it in silence for a moment, his hands clasped behind his back, his coat buttons straining across his belly. "He was truly a talent, wasn't he? I might even use the term 'genius.'" He turned to look at Olive. "I don't suppose you would permit me to enter one of the paintings, would you, Olive? As a magical academic, I find these living works of the utmost interest, both compositionally and historically . . ."

Inside of Olive's collar, the spectacles seemed to flare with a sudden chill. It didn't feel right to say no to grown-ups—especially to grown-ups who were trying to help her—but the thought of Doctor Widdecombe squishing his body into those frames and strutting through those painted worlds made Olive want to shove him off the porch and send him rolling down Linden Street like a big tweed bowling ball. "Um . . . maybe another time," she said. "After we've finished searching the house." She turned toward the doors. "Shouldn't we be—"

"Doctor Widdecombe," Rutherford interrupted, "have any other practitioners of magic used paint the way Aldous McMartin did, to create or trap living beings?"

Olive sent Rutherford an impatient look, but Rutherford was too busy watching Doctor Widdecombe to notice.

"None so successfully as Aldous McMartin," said Doctor Widdecombe sagely. "A few have tried and failed. A witch named Fiona Albumblatt experimented with moving ink in the early nineteenth century, but this just meant that all of her spells scrambled themselves after she wrote them down. And of course magicians have worked with living clay for years: golems, dolls, and so forth. But none was an artist like Aldous McMartin. He was in a category of his own."

Olive felt the back of her neck begin to prickle. She glanced around. Mrs. Dewey was watching her with a sympathetic expression.

"Shall we move along?" Mrs. Dewey asked, giving Olive's shoulder a sweet-scented pat.

"What do you think, Delora, my love?" asked Doctor Widdecombe.

Delora flowed to the center of the room. She raised her hands, closed her eyes, and made a series of wobbly turns, like a sleep-deprived ballerina.

Olive heard Mrs. Dewey give a little sigh.

"Yes," Delora whispered. "The secret of their power is not here."

"Let's carry on," said Doctor Widdecombe. "Olive, lead the way."

Olive darted into the hall. The others trailed unhurriedly behind her.

They dragged through the formal parlor—the cold, frilly room where Annabelle had sat while her grandfather painted her portrait, many decades ago—and then into the high-ceilinged dining room, moving so slowly that Olive thought her skeleton might pop out of her skin and run restlessly ahead. Walter gazed around, silent and bug-eyed. Delora sniffed and pawed at the air. Doctor Widdecombe pressed his nose right up to every shelf and photograph and cabinet and painting, like someone visiting a museum. When they finally reached the kitchen, he even began pulling out the drawers, removing objects and holding them up to the light.

"How interesting!" he announced, lifting an antique device that might have been a cheese slicer or a comb for someone with extremely thin hair. "And pickle tongs! Fascinating! This is truly a McMartin time capsule!" he exclaimed, while Olive's toes tapped faster and faster on the floor. "Olive, I'm sure my enthusiasm seems extreme, but for a historian like myself, this is equivalent to a private tour of Windsor Castle—or of Pharaoh Tutankhamen's tomb!"

"His tomb?" Olive repeated, with an unpleasant little wrench in her stomach.

"If you would permit me, Olive," said Doctor Widdecombe, picking up what looked like a tiny pizza cutter with ruffled edges, "I would like to write an article about this house for *The Abracademic Magicologist*. I'm a frequent contributor, and I'm certain that—"

"Hush!" breathed Delora. Her voice was just a whisper, but everyone obeyed. "Do you hear?"

"Hear what, Aunt Delora?" Walter prompted, hovering anxiously behind her.

"Hush!" Delora commanded again.

"Why ask questions if you don't want any answers?" asked Mrs. Dewey, sounding slightly annoyed.

But Delora didn't seem to hear. With her eyes closed, she sashayed between the countertops, both hands batting the air before her face as if she were being swarmed by invisible bees.

"Delora's gift is very sensitive," Doctor Widdecombe murmured, watching his ladylove swat at the empty air. "It needs silence and patience in which to make itself known."

Everyone watched, keeping quiet, as Delora spun slowly around and nearly smacked into the refrigerator.

"It is near," she breathed, her eyes still closed. Her hands patted at the refrigerator door. "Darkness. Great, great power."

Olive glanced at Rutherford. He was staring at Delora intently, his whole body craning in her direction. Olive knew he was trying to read Delora's mind, but with her eyes closed, he was finding it very hard. What would the inside of a mind like Delora's look like, anyway? Olive pictured a cemetery where, instead of graves, there were rows and rows of ringing telephones.

"Lead us, my love," whispered Doctor Widdecombe. "Be our guide."

Delora hesitated, her body swiveling from side to side like a black velvet satellite dish. Then, with her head turned toward the house's interior, she froze. Her eyes popped open. "This way," she announced.

Delora streaked across the kitchen, sleek black hair flying behind her. The others hurried after. Before any of them could catch up, Delora had thrown open the basement door.

A breath of air, colder than the autumn winds outside, floated up from the darkness. The group clustered in the doorway. The ancient wooden steps below them seemed to dwindle down into nothing, erased by blackness before they could reach the floor.

Without another word, Delora plunged down the steps. In a moment, she too had vanished into the dark.

"Be careful, my love!" Doctor Widdecombe called, setting a tentative toe on the first step. The wood groaned loudly. "These stairs do not look structurally sound!"

"There's a light at the bottom of the steps!" called Olive at the same time.

But both of their words were lost in the rising wave of Delora's scream.

E VERYONE GALLOPED DOWN the basement stairs.
"Delora, darling!" cried Doctor Widdecombe,
taking the lead. He teetered heroically down the
squealing steps. "Are you all right? Speak to me!"

"We're coming, Aunt Delora!" Walter rumbled
from the back of the crowd.

"What on earth?" puffed Mrs. Dewey, who was
squished in the middle between Olive and Rutherford.

The basement was too dark to see Delora, or whatever it was that had made her scream. Standing on her
toes, Olive grabbed the chain of the hanging lightbulb. Its yellow glow pushed the blackness into the
corners, uncovering the cobwebbed rafters, the dusty,
junk-strewn shelves, and the cold, uneven stone walls.
Patches of flaking plaster clung here and there. Mortar

crumbled between the stones like very old cheese in a very old sandwich.

In one corner where the darkness never quite disappeared, a pair of bright green eyes glittered, and Olive knew that Leopold was in his station atop the trapdoor. Olive also knew that the trapdoor led to a dirt-walled tunnel, which wound its way to the hidden stone room where Aldous had concocted his paints. Aldous's ingredients—bony, oily, powdery, and sometimes many-legged—still waited there in rows of foggy glass jars. Olive knew firsthand that trying to create and use these paints could be disastrous. The thought of Doctor Widdecombe or Delora or even Mrs. Dewey finding out about them made Olive's heart sink like a sponge soaked in ice water.

But, fortunately, it wasn't the trapdoor that had caught Delora's attention.

Delora stood in a corner near the washing machine, swaying slowly back and forth.

"Delora, my precious rose, what is it?" Doctor Widdecombe asked—although Olive noticed that he stopped several steps away from where his rose was currently planted.

"It is here," Delora whispered. "I could feel it, branching up through the entire house." She spread her hands toward the stone wall. "The cold! The power! The root of the darkness!"

Doctor Widdecombe edged toward the wall. His knees creaked as he bent down. "'Aillil McMartin. Angus McMartin, 1793.'" He straightened up again so suddenly that everyone else jumped. "Of course!" he announced. "These are *gravestones*! Argyle and Athdar and Alastair McMartin—it must be the entire McMartin line!"

"Yes," said Olive. "I know."

Doctor Widdecombe wheeled around. "You know?" he repeated.

"Back in Scotland, when their neighbors destroyed the McMartin home, Aldous saved all the bits of the family plot that hadn't been wrecked," she said, repeating the story that the cats had once told her, what already felt like a century ago. "So he took the gravestones and . . . everything that had been under them. And then he brought them here."

"Graves?" Walter's deep voice wobbled. "Doesn't that—mmm—doesn't that bother you? Knowing they're down here? In your house?"

Olive tried to recall how she'd felt when she first discovered the gravestones, in the dim basement, under the watchful eye of a huge black cat. It hadn't been pleasant, she was sure. But over time the gravestones had become just one more strange thing in a house full of strange things. At least the gravestones had never climbed down from the walls and tried to drown her.

"They're only gravestones," she said, sounding braver than she felt. "They can't do anything."

"I'm afraid that you are wrong," said Doctor Widdecombe. "Come closer, Olive. Look."

Olive edged across the basement toward Doctor Widdecombe. She bent over beside him, bringing her own face nearer to the crumbling stone wall.

"Do you see what is happening here?" Doctor Widdecombe asked.

Olive squinted. "I guess that *Athdar* one looks a little bit crumblier than before. But that might be because the dryer wobbles and hits it sometimes."

"Not their texture," said Doctor Widdecombe. "Their color."

Olive squinted at the wall again. Where the gravestones had once been a dirty grayish brown, now they were more of a brownish gray. Or a blackish gray. Or just black.

"They are quite a different color from the rest of the stones, wouldn't you agree?" prompted Doctor Widdecombe.

Olive nodded, frowning. Over her shoulder, she glanced at the green eyes gleaming from the darkness.

"Next, note the temperature," Doctor Widdecombe went on, as though they were examining a specimen in a laboratory. "It's rather unsettlingly low."

"The walls are always cold," said Olive.

"*This* cold?" Doctor Widdecombe took her gently

by the wrist and pressed her palm to Angus McMartin's headstone.

The shock was so immediate and so strong that at first Olive couldn't tell if her skin was freezing or burning. She jerked her arm away. A print of her hand, as clear as if her palm had been coated in paint, smoked against the surface of the stone, a deeper black against the dark gray. It faded swiftly away again.

"*This* is what the McMartins want back," Doctor Widdecombe said authoritatively. He turned to look at the others, his voice ringing through the stone room. "A constant source of power. A link straight through the past, to the magic of each ancestor, the identities preserved to feed and fuel all the heirs to come. I have heard of this before, in other magical families—but never have I seen such a large or perfect collection."

"Why is it changing now?" Olive asked, holding her still-prickling hand against her side.

"Imagine a reservoir," said Doctor Widdecombe, shaping his meaty hands into a bowl. "Over time, the pool fills with rain, rising higher and higher. But no one uses the water inside. At last the water grows so high, its mass so huge, that it overflows—or it seeps through the walls around it, weakening and rotting everything that it can reach." Slowly, Doctor Widdecombe spread his fingers. The bowl disintegrated.

Horatio's words—*The McMartins are seeking someone to train. Someone to take on this house*—floated back through

Olive's mind. "The house is looking for an heir," she said softly. "It needs someone to use its power."

Doctor Widdecombe gave an admiring nod. "Precisely," he said. "And it is growing stronger with each passing moment."

Delora lunged across the room. "Olive, you must get out of here!" she cried, grabbing Olive by both shoulders. "That it hasn't corrupted you already is astonishing! The McMartins will never leave you in peace," she breathed, her silvery eyes staring straight into Olive's. "Not as long as you remain in this house!"

Once more, Olive glanced over her shoulder. The green eyes stared steadily from their corner.

The cats needed her. She couldn't leave them to face the McMartins alone, not when the danger was Olive's own fault. And Morton, and all of the people inside Elsewhere . . .

"But I can't leave," she told everyone. "I *can't*."

Doctor Widdecombe stepped forward. "Olive, your safety is at greater risk with every second you stay here."

"But I don't—"

"You must get away from this place!" Delora shrieked, her hands tightening around Olive's arms until Olive winced. "Get away! *Leave this house!*"

A black streak shot through the gloom and planted itself before Olive's feet.

"I will ask you to remove your hands from Miss Olive, madam," Leopold boomed, making himself so rigid that the tips of his ears reached well above Olive's knees.

Delora blinked as if she'd just woken from a daydream. Her grip slid weakly from Olive's arms.

Leopold remained in place, glaring up at Delora.

"Leopold," Olive asked, "didn't you notice that the gravestones were changing?"

Leopold's eyes flicked warily around the room. "That is classified information, miss." His voice dropped to a whisper. "And I suspect that we are *not alone.*"

"It's all right," said Olive. "Please tell us."

Leopold's chest inflated still further. He raised his chin. "Very well, miss. It is correct that the stones have altered. Observation, rather than action, has been our chosen course."

"Why didn't you tell me?"

"Why *would* we tell you?" Leopold asked, looking surprised. "There is nothing to be done. The stones have changed many times over the years. They've altered very frequently over the course of the past few months, as Annabelle, and Aldous . . . and *you,*" Leopold added, under his breath, "have used the house's powers."

"What about lately? Have they gotten better?"

"Yes. Better," Leopold said. "And then worse again. And then . . ."

"And then what?"

Leopold blinked. "Even worse."

"And so the guard on the wall watches the water rise and does nothing," said Doctor Widdecombe. "It rises so very slowly, after all—until, very slowly, it rises over the wall, and floods the entire town."

Leopold's chest rose until it bumped into his chin. "I don't believe you are a member of this brigade, sir," he said tightly.

Doctor Widdecombe turned to Olive. "Under these circumstances, it would be neither wise nor kind of us to allow you to remain here until the danger is removed."

"Removed?" Rutherford piped up. "Are you suggesting extricating the gravestones from the foundation? Because I think that might seriously damage the house's structural—"

"No," Delora cut him off. Her mirror-like eyes traveled up to Doctor Widdecombe's face, then glided through the darkness to land on Mrs. Dewey. "But there are ways."

"What ways?" asked Olive.

Delora's mouth opened, but it was Mrs. Dewey's voice that spoke next.

"Absolutely not." Her tone was sharp enough to slice bread. She stepped into the center of the chilly room, folding her arms across her chest. "We will not do anything so risky or reprehensible. It goes against everything we stand for."

Delora raised her hands warningly. "You ignore my warning at your own peril, Lydia."

"I think I'll take my chances, *Debbie.*"

Delora jerked back as though Mrs. Dewey had yanked a hair out of her nose.

"That's right," Mrs. Dewey went on. "I remember when you were still just Deborah Schepkey from Cleveland."

"Cleveland?" Doctor Widdecombe's eyebrows rose. "You told me that you were raised in the Northeast by a band of traveling fortune-tellers."

"If you—*any* of you—feel so terribly threatened by what might be contained in this house," Mrs. Dewey resumed, before Delora could get her gaping mouth to work, "then why don't you leave it?"

"But—" Olive interrupted. "What about what Delora said? Why—"

"Lydia is right, my black dove," said Doctor Widdecombe, putting his hand gently on Delora's arm. He didn't seem to hear Olive at all. "It would behoove us all to calm ourselves and collect our thoughts. This sort of arguing is unworthy of us. We shall depart." He ushered his wife toward the staircase. "Walter?"

"I think—I think I'll stay here," said Walter. His deep voice echoed against the stones. "For a little while."

Doctor Widdecombe shook his head. "To each his own," he said, as though Walter had just ordered oatmeal at an ice cream parlor. He and Delora creaked up the steps into the daylight.

"May I go with them, Grandma?" Rutherford asked, darting after. "Not because I'm afraid of this house," he added, "but because I'd like to ask Doctor Widdecombe some questions about protective charms."

"You may," said Mrs. Dewey.

Rutherford scampered up the stairs.

Mrs. Dewey let out a breath. She looked from Walter to Olive, her mouth forming a tiny smile. "Now," she said, "why don't you two join me for a little lunch?"

In the kitchen of the old stone house, grayish daylight wound its way through the vine-covered windows. Patches of light gleamed on the worn wooden table and glittered in the cups of Mrs. Dewey's steaming tea. Olive stirred several sugar cubes into hers. Walter sipped his tentatively, his long, knobby fingers forming a complete loop around the cup.

"Is—mmm—is there Matchstick Mallow in this?" he asked.

Mrs. Dewey's little pink smile widened. "Very good," she said. "You must know your infusions."

Walter shook his head. "No," he said. "No. I don't. I just—I just read a lot."

Olive took a drink of her tea. She thought she could feel her heart beating a bit more solidly, the slump of her spine starting to straighten. It could have used a few more sugar cubes, but the tea was making her feel a bit braver, anyway.

"Mrs. Dewey?" she asked, reaching for another slice of Mrs. Dewey's frosted pound cake.

"Yes, Olive?"

"The thing that Delora said—about removing the root of the power?"

Mrs. Dewey's face tightened. "Yes?"

"Why shouldn't we try it?"

"Because, Olive, that sort of magic is precisely the things that the S.M.U.D.S. hopes to stamp out. It's dark, dangerous, nasty stuff. And it has the potential to go dangerously, nastily wrong."

"But what if it went *right*?" Olive persisted. "We might be able to get rid of Annabelle and Aldous and get my parents back all at the same time!"

Mrs. Dewey picked up a crumb that had landed near Olive's elbow. "Just because it takes time and skill to bake a cake, should we give up on baking cakes completely?" Mrs. Dewey asked. "Should we eat raw eggs and spoonfuls of flour and sugar instead? Should we just put birthday candles in a stick of butter?"

". . . No," said Olive, biting into her third slice and thinking of how sad a world without cakes would be.

"The same things are needed here," said Mrs. Dewey. "Time and skill."

"Okay." Olive took a gulp of tea. "Then what if we just called Annabelle here, right now, and offered her whatever she wants in exchange for my parents?"

Mrs. Dewey looked at Olive sharply. She tugged the teacup out of Olive's hands. "If we wait for Annabelle to turn up on her own, we'll have the upper hand. If we seem desperate, it will show her how much power she has."

Olive thumped her heels impatiently against the legs of her chair. "So what do we do next?"

"Well," said Mrs. Dewey, setting down her own teacup with a delicate click, "Byron and Delora and I will continue our work together—once I make peace with Delora, that is. She really *is* a gifted messenger, even if she is a flake." Her eyes shot to the other side of the table. "Don't tell your aunt I said that, Walter."

Walter hid a grin behind his steaming teacup.

"We will try to find your parents without confronting Annabelle. If she feels threatened, it's more likely that she'll do something . . . permanent." Mrs. Dewey stirred her tea, looking down.

"But what about me?" Olive insisted. "What can *I* do?"

"You can go to school," said Mrs. Dewey.

Olive's jaw nearly hit the table. *"School?"*

"Tomorrow is the start of a new school week. Unless we want teachers calling and truancy officers turning up at the front door, you will have to go to school and behave as normally as possible. I'll call the university and explain that your parents have come down with a nasty flu, and they may not be back for several days." Mrs. Dewey leaned closer to Olive, her soft, round face eclipsing the rest of the room. "But they *will* be back, Olive," she said softly. "They'll be home, safe and sound, before you know it. And, until they are," Mrs. Dewey went on, sitting back in her chair again, "if you're sure you want to stay in this house, I insist that you have someone stay here with you. A *grown-up, human* someone," she added, before Olive could argue. "Whomever you choose will be your guest, Olive. This is still your home." She gave Olive's hand a powdery pat. "Personally, I would be glad to stay with you."

Olive looked into Mrs. Dewey's crinkly eyes. They were warm and familiar and kind—and still, Horatio's words about the house wanting an heir seemed to taint them with something colder. As good as Doctor Widdecombe or Delora or even Mrs. Dewey and Rutherford might be, couldn't they be corrupted? If the house had managed to turn Olive against her own best friends—at least for a little while—what might it do to someone who could actually *use* its power? The only guest who could be trusted would be someone like Olive herself, who didn't have any natural magical talent. Someone like—

"Walter," said Olive. "Just Walter can stay."

Walter gave a little start. The tea sloshed in his cup. "Me?" He blinked at Olive, his eyes eager and even wider than usual. "Really?" His Adam's apple bobbed as he forced his voice back to a lower pitch. "I mean—thank you, Olive. I want to help in any way I can."

Olive gave Walter a nod. Then she glanced at Mrs. Dewey, who was clearing the lunch things, her face set in a pleasant little smile. Nobody was going to take this house away from her. Not an enemy. Not a friend. No one.

THAT AFTERNOON, WALTER moved a lumpy
brown bag of his things into the old stone house.
He and Olive rattled uncomfortably around the empty
rooms for the next few hours, each of them keeping an
eye on the other while trying to look like they weren't
doing just that. To Olive, it felt almost like having a
babysitter—which would have been embarrassing
enough—but instead of a chirpy, bossy high-schooler,
she had *Walter,* a slow, seven-foot, sub-par sorcerer
with a voice like a congested walrus.

For dinner that night, Walter made grilled cheese
sandwiches that were less *grilled* than *immolated,* and
less *sandwiches* than *crumbly black lumps.* They sat at the
kitchen table in awkward quiet, Walter crunching
away at his crumbly black lump, and Olive crumbling

hers into smaller black lumps that landed with loud *clacks* on her dinner plate. Their reflections hung in the darkened window, between Mr. and Mrs. Dunwoody's empty chairs.

"Thank you for dinner, Walter," Olive said as soon as she'd demolished the last of her food. She tipped its remains down the kitchen sink before sidling toward the hall. "I'm going up to my room. I have some homework to finish for tomorrow."

Walter blinked at her from across the table, his long, bony arms braced to bring the burnt sandwich to his mouth. "Okay," he rumbled.

"You can read books in the library, if you want," Olive added, trying to seem less unfriendly. "Or watch TV in the living room."

"TV?" Walter's eyes widened. "I haven't watched television since—mmm—not since I moved in with Aunt Delora. She says a screen can't compete with what she sees and hears in her head all the time." Walter swallowed. "But I *like* screens." He straightened up eagerly, his neck stretching up from his collar like a plant in a pot. "Is *We Will Wok You* still on?"

"I don't know," said Olive, backing into the hall. "Maybe."

By the time she'd reached the staircase, she could hear the TV blaring.

Olive ran up the steps to her bedroom. After grabbing a pack of cards from her dresser drawer, she zipped back out into the hall, put on the spectacles, and dove into the painting of Linden Street.

"Are we going to dance in the ballroom?" Morton asked as Olive led him hurriedly back down the hill. "Or visit Baltus and the masons?"

"We can't go downstairs," Olive explained, grabbing the picture frame that hung before them in the misty air. "Walter is staying here, and I don't want him trying to tag along. Besides, there's somebody else we should visit."

Inside his painted gazebo, Roberto the Magnificent hopped to his feet.

"Back for a repeat performance?" he shouted as Olive and Morton climbed through the frame. "Presto!" The bouquet shot all the way out of his sleeve this time, zooming a few feet into the air before flying back toward his arm and disappearing with a noise like a crumpling can.

"Well, dang," said the lanky man, peering up his sleeve. "Just when I thought I had it working again..."

Morton stared, wide-eyed, at the magician. "*You* didn't live in this neighborhood," he said. "I would remember."

"No sirree," the man answered. "I came to town with Binkle and Rudd's World-Wandering Carnival.

Roberto the Magnificent," he added, giving Morton a grand bow. "That's 'Robert,' to you." With a flourish, he waved one hand past Morton's ear, then frowned down at his empty fingers. "Now where the heck did that coin go?" he muttered.

"Aldous McMartin himself trapped both of you here, so you must have been . . . um . . . *alive* at close to the same time," said Olive as delicately as she could. "I thought Morton might know something about the 'others' you mentioned."

"Other weirdos?" Morton asked, watching Robert dig through his many pockets.

"Other magicians," said Robert. Triumphantly, he swept a blue handkerchief out of his vest, which led to a red handkerchief, and then an emerald handkerchief, and then zipped itself inward like a mechanical tape measure. Robert sighed.

"The old man showed up at the fairgrounds, after the carnival was closed down for the night," he began. "I was in my trailer, and all at once he was there too—that tall, bony body just looming over me. I never even heard the door open."

"What did he say to you?" Olive whispered, even though no one was around to hear.

"He said—he said he was getting rid of all the other magicians. When he was done, there'd be no one left but his own family. I told him, 'I just do tricks, that's all,' but . . ." Robert trailed off with a shrug.

"Did he say anything else about those other magicians? Where he'd put them, or what their names were, or—"

Robert was already shaking his head. "I don't believe so. Sorry."

"What do you think, Morton?" Olive asked.

"I think he needs to practice his tricks some more," said Morton as Robert finally found the coin in his pants pocket, shouted "Ah-ha!" and promptly dropped it into his pants again.

"I mean about Aldous trapping other magicians. Do you think there might have been other magicians . . . or witches . . . on your street?"

"No," said Morton. His face began to look worried. "And the Old Man trapped lots of good, normal people too. My parents are normal. Your parents are normal. Sort of."

"But what if it was a secret?" Olive persisted. "The McMartins tried to keep their powers hidden. I wasn't supposed to know about Mrs. Dewey, or—"

Morton balled his fists. "My parents wouldn't keep secrets from me," he said angrily.

"I didn't mean—"

"It's not a secret!" Morton shouted. "But you're not supposed to talk about it!"

"Morton, wait!" Olive called as Morton stomped off toward the frame. She shoved the pack of playing cards into Robert's hand. "These aren't paint, so they might

work better in here," she said, heading after Morton's billowing nightshirt. "Bye!"

"Good-bye!" Robert shouted after her. "Come back anytime! All shows are free!"

Morton was waiting for her by the frame, his chin tucked to his chest.

Olive took him by the arm. Together, they climbed out of the painting, landing softly on the bedroom floor.

"What did you mean?" Olive whispered as they slipped back into the hall, Morton leading the way. "That we're not supposed to talk about it?"

Morton threw her an exasperated look. "We're not supposed to *talk about it!*" he hissed back. His eyes flicked around the darkening hallway. "They'll hear you!"

"But the McMartins are gone."

Morton halted in front of the painting of Linden Street, refusing to speak until Olive took his arm again and pulled him through the frame.

"They're never really gone," he muttered, once they were safe on the other side, sprawling in the dewy grass. He wriggled his arm out of Olive's grip.

"Maybe we could ask your neighbors about magic, just to make sure," said Olive, getting to her feet.

"You can ask them," said Morton. He strode ahead of her up the hillside. "I already know the answer."

Candles glowed softly from inside closed windows as Olive and Morton hurried along the street. In dark second-floor bedrooms, curtains twitched as they passed by. Olive glanced up at the house next to Morton's—the house that belonged to Mrs. Dewey inside the real world—and spotted an old lady in a ruffled nightcap rocking very slowly back and forth in a rocking chair on the porch.

"Hello," called Olive.

"Evening," said the woman.

"I don't mean to bother you," Olive began, "but we wondered if we could ask you something."

"She means if *she* could ask you something," Morton corrected.

The woman went on rocking softly. "You may," she said.

"Thank you. Um, you wouldn't happen to be a—I mean, Aldous McMartin didn't have any reason to think you were a *witch,* did he?"

The chair stopped rocking. The woman didn't answer.

"I mean," Olive struggled on, "maybe you used magic, or you knew something about it that—"

"'Knew something'?" the woman interrupted in a hushed voice. "The only thing I knew about magic was that it was safest to know *nothing about it.*" Tugging her shawl around her body, she stood up and went swiftly into her house. The door pulled itself shut behind her.

"I told you," Morton muttered.

"And what are you two up to now?" asked a voice from behind them.

Olive and Morton spun around.

An old man with a long, crinkly beard strolled toward them across the deserted street. Mist rippled around the cuffs of his pajamas.

"Hello, Mr. Fitzroy," said Olive politely. "We were just asking—"

"*She* was just asking," Morton interrupted.

"I was asking if anyone else in this neighborhood had . . . powers. Like Aldous McMartin." Olive swallowed, looking up into the man's stern face. "If he might have thought that any of you could use magic. If he thought you were a threat."

"No," said the old man. Beneath his bushy eyebrows, his paint-flecked eyes shuttled between Olive and Morton. "None of *us* were." He folded his arms. "And I doubt you'll find anyone here willing to talk to you about magic. We all learned that lesson."

"Oh," said Olive softly, looking away from the old man's painted eyes.

"But I will tell you this." Mr. Fitzroy bent closer, lowering his voice. "*Like draws like.* More than a few secrets were kept on this street." He glanced up at the unchanging twilit sky, as though he were still expecting it to flood with the darkness of Aldous's presence.

"Now," he resumed, firmly changing the subject, "why don't you two join me for a game of horseshoes?"

"You have horseshoes?" asked Morton eagerly.

"I have *a* horseshoe, and I've got a fencepost. Sometimes the horseshoe hits it before it flies back."

"Thank you, but I'm going to keep looking," said Olive. "Bye, Morton," she called over her shoulder, but Morton was already trotting across the street with Mr. Fitzroy, his long white nightshirt flickering in the dimness.

Back in the upstairs hallway, Olive took a frustrated look around. The sky beyond the windows was black. It was well past her usual bedtime. The sound of the television rose up the stairs, clicking knives and hissing woks mixing with rumbles of dramatic music. Olive sat down on the top step and joggled both legs impatiently. How could she possibly go into her bedroom and try to fall asleep, as though this was an ordinary night? She had to do *something*—something that would bring her closer to learning the truth.

. . . More than a few secrets were kept on this street.

There were *still* plenty of secrets on Linden Street, Olive thought angrily. There were the secrets in her own house, and in Mrs. Nivens's house, and in Mrs. Dewey's house—

Olive clamped her hands around her knees to hold them still. She could search Linden Street *herself*! Mrs.

Dewey and the Widdecombes hadn't found any clues there, but that didn't mean there was nothing to find. Olive shot to her feet. Maybe she would spot something that they had missed.

For a moment, she considered asking someone else to go with her—one of the cats, or Morton and his neighbors. Then she pictured Morton's neighbors set loose on the street, pressing their painted faces to the windows of their own former houses, giving Mr. Fergus and the Butlers and Mr. Hanniman simultaneous heart attacks.

No. Like Horatio had said, any time a secret is shared, it grows less safe. It would be better if she went alone. But she couldn't go down the stairs and out the door without explaining herself to Walter. She would have to take another route.

Inside her own bedroom, Olive lifted the heavy wooden window frame and slipped out onto the balcony. It was a tiny space, no bigger than a fire escape, but the branches of the ash tree enclosed it on all sides, reaching out to Olive with their long, bare arms.

Olive made sure that her flashlight was secure in her pocket. She buttoned her black sweater all the way to her chin. Then, cautiously, she threw one leg over the wrought iron railing and wrapped both arms around the nearest sturdy branch. Hanging on tight, Olive kicked away from the balcony and swung her right leg up and over, so that she was stretched along the branch like a big, clumsy panther. The branch bounced softly under her.

Shimmying backward, making sure not to crush the spectacles, Olive moved along the branch to the trunk. From there, it was just two short jumps to the ground.

Olive landed in a pile of crackling leaves. She brushed her bark-scratched palms together and surveyed the backyard. The lawn was perfectly still. The bluish light of the TV pulsed behind the living room windows, flickering over the withered garden.

Keeping low, Olive edged around the old stone house. She would save the Dewey and Nivens houses for last, to postpone the chance of being spotted. She darted to the right, to the far side of the old stone house, crawling between the dry ferns and overgrown shrub roses into the front yard.

The sky was overcast, a sheet of dark gray clouds obscuring the moon. The weak glow of the streetlights outlined the Halloween headstones still scattered across the lawn. The sight of them made Olive catch her breath. She thought of the gravestones in the basement, the freezing shock of her hand against the wall. She thought of the headstones in the painting of the Scottish hills, *Mother* and *Father* carved on their silent faces. Shuddering, she darted forward, keeping her eyes fixed on the silent street.

Before she'd passed the first row of headstones, something lurched out from between the graves. Olive froze, dropping to the ground. The figure lumbered forward. It was tall—so tall that it hardly seemed human—and it headed directly toward her, in long, deliberate steps.

"Olive?" said a deep voice. "Mmm . . . What are you doing out here?"

"Walter!" Olive squeaked.

"Where are you going?"

"Nowhere," said Olive, inching backward. A foam headstone bumped her in the side. "I was—I was just going to look for my parents."

"The S.M.U.D.S. has already checked the whole street."

"I know, but I thought I might—"

Walter's black silhouette towered over her, moving closer. "This isn't safe. It's my job to guard you. And the only places you're allowed to be are *school* and *home*."

"But—"

"Sorry." The bony shoulders of Walter's silhouette went up and down. "These are the rules. I have to keep you safe. Now, let's go back inside."

Olive let out a shaky breath. Slowly, she rose to her feet and headed toward the old stone house. Walter's watchful presence loomed behind her.

She slumped up the staircase to her room. As she

climbed, she could hear Walter turning the locks of the front door, checking the windows, making sure everything was secure. The walls of the stone house loomed around her, solid and watchful. For the first time, Olive realized that being *protected* and being *trapped* could feel like the very same thing.

"I KNEW THAT MABEL was on her way out, but Dun-
stan..." Ms. Teedlebaum shook her head sadly. Her
red hair, still stiff with wood glue, shook too. "Dun-
stan came as a complete shock. I'd nursed him back to
health, played his favorite bagpipe music, read to him
from *The Joy of Cooking*... It was his favorite book. And
still, last night..." Ms. Teedlebaum sighed. "I've told
myself again and again, 'This is the last time, Florence.
Spider plants are one thing, but you get too attached
to ferns. You can't keep putting yourself through this.'
But then you see another fern just waiting for you in
its little pot, and it looks so friendly and hopeful..."
Ms. Teedlebaum sighed again, brushing a tear from
the corner of her eye. "I just don't know how Graciela
and Howard are going to pull through."

At the front of the classroom, the girl with the eyeliner raised her hand. "Are Graciela and Howard houseplants too?"

Ms. Teedlebaum waved her paint-flecked fingers dismissively. "Of course not. They're goldfish. Ooh, that reminds me." She uncapped one of the pens dangling from cords around her neck and jotted in one of the notepads that hung nearby. "'Four codfish filets.'"

Capping the pen again, Ms. Teedlebaum gazed around the classroom of staring students. "Now—what were we working on? Oh, yes. Collages." She gave a happier sigh. "Aren't collages marvelous? They're so relaxing, especially when you're a highly organized person, like me." The art teacher slid down from her stool with a clatter of keys and pens and necklaces. "All right, everyone. Find your materials and get started."

With the rest of the class, Olive trudged to the cabinets and pulled down her collage. It was supposed to be an almost-finished outdoor scene, but instead it was a far-from-finished mess. Olive couldn't keep her mind on her work. All week, she had dragged herself through the school days, doing meaningless assignments and gluing meaningless bits of paper to a meaningless art project, while the sadness and guilt that sloshed inside of her boiled down into something dry and volatile, like the powder inside of a firecracker. One spark and she would come flying apart.

Olive leaned her head on one clenched fist and glared down at her collage. The sliver of her brain that hoped that her parents would return on their own, safe and sound, had been snipped down to nothing. There was no room for patience. There was no room for art class, or homework, or picking at meals alone with Walter in the quiet stone house. In fact, Walter was driving Olive batty. From the moment she got home from school until the moment she went to bed, Walter watched her, lurking around corners, too big to be truly sneaky. At night, after Olive was meant to be asleep, she could hear his steps creaking along the upper hall, pausing outside her closed bedroom door. Listening.

The people who were supposed to be helping her hadn't been any help at all, Olive realized. Inside of her, a spark began to snap and fizzle. How much longer did they expect her to shuffle obediently back and forth from school to the house, wasting her time on art projects and—

A swinging clump of keys smacked Olive between the shoulder blades.

"Are you all right, Olive?" Ms. Teedlebaum asked. She craned over the side of Olive's high white table, her bangle bracelets jangling. "You look like something is bothering you."

"I'm fine," said Olive, as calmly as she could. "Thank you."

"My story didn't upset you, did it?" Ms. Teedlebaum lowered her voice. "Have you lost a houseplant yourself recently?"

"No. I haven't lost any houseplants."

"Good," said Ms. Teedlebaum. She turned to focus on Olive's collage, and a corkscrew of red hair, smelling faintly of wood glue, tickled Olive's cheek. "This is very interesting work, Olive. You have a unique way of looking at the world. That's just what an artist needs: That vision, and a way to capture it."

With those words, Ms. Teedlebaum sailed away on a jingle of keys, leaving Olive chewing on the inside of her cheek. She fought down the sudden, strong urge to tear up her collage, rip that captured image into bits, and set it free into the chilly wind that roared past the classroom windows.

The instant she and Rutherford had climbed off the bus at the foot of Linden Street, Olive whirled around and grabbed Rutherford by the sleeve. "What are they going to do tonight?" she asked urgently. "Your grandmother and the others?"

Rutherford looked vaguely surprised to find Olive's fingers wrapped around his arm. "They are making progress," he said, blinking back at her. "My grandmother says that they haven't found definitive proof of where your parents might be, but they've eliminated several possibilities."

A gust of cool autumn wind swept down the hill. Olive scowled at the leaves that flung themselves against her jacket, like a hundred little hands trying to push her backward. "What about Annabelle?" she asked, dropping Rutherford's sleeve. "Do they know if she's alone, or if she freed Aldous somehow, or if she's working with someone else? *Anything?*"

"They have not drawn any conclusions on that matter," said Rutherford.

"But it's been *days*. Why is it taking so long?"

Rutherford blinked at her through his smudgy glasses. "They are trying to help while maintaining the safety of everyone involved, Olive."

"I know. But, I just—" Olive clenched her teeth, imagining a miniature Annabelle between her molars. "I just want to *do* something. I can't wait any more."

"I understand." Rutherford's face brightened. "Perhaps you should join us for dinner this evening. Walter could watch the house, and you and I could play chess. Or we could set up my new figurines for a reenactment of the War of the Roses."

Olive shook her head. "I would, but if I even go out to the yard, Walter follows me."

They had reached the lawn of the Nivens house.

Olive slowed her steps, glancing up at the lifeless windows looming above them. "Are you sure we can trust him, Rutherford?" she asked. "I know he's not a real witch, and the cats would never let him use any of the house's secrets—if he could even figure out *how*—but I hate leaving him there while I'm gone. Yesterday, when I came home, I found him picking through the dead plants in the garden. And on Wednesday, he asked me if there's a root cellar under the basement. He must have noticed the trapdoor. Do you really think he's safe?"

Rutherford halted. He turned to stare at Olive. "You're asking me if I think *Walter* is *dangerous*?" he asked. "I think a baby rabbit with a sleep disorder would pose more of a threat." Olive pictured a tiny rabbit in a turtleneck flopping down with a snore on the library rug. She giggled in spite of herself. Rutherford tilted his head to one side. "You need to trust people sometimes, Olive."

Olive sighed. She wrapped both arms tight around herself and felt the spectacles digging into her skin. "But sometimes I've trusted the wrong people."

They were quiet for a moment. Through the broken window of Lucinda Nivens's abandoned bedroom, the curtains gave a ghostly twitch. Olive shivered.

"Did you say something?" Rutherford asked abruptly.

"When?"

"Just now."

"I said, 'Sometimes I've trusted the wrong people.'"

"After that." Rutherford blinked. "I thought I heard you say something about parabolic equations."

"I don't think I've ever said *anything* about parabolic equations," said Olive. "Except right now." She smiled, thinking how happy her parents would be if they knew she had even used the words *parabolic equations* . . . and then her lips began to tremble. She wheeled back to the sidewalk, striding toward the old stone house. Rutherford hurried to keep up.

"Tonight, I'm going to do something myself," said Olive as they climbed the creaking porch steps. The cold that radiated from the walls swirled over them, enveloping them in its chilly breath. "Maybe I'll sneak out of the house, maybe I'll get the cats to help me search; I don't know. But I have to do *something*." She glanced at Rutherford. "You can come with me, or not—but don't tell anyone. Please."

Rutherford nodded solemnly. "I will consider your proposal," he said. "And my secrecy is assured."

"Good." Through the windows to her left, Olive could see a twitch of motion as a dark, skinny figure scurried past the glass. Walter was in the library. An anxious feeling began to spread like a burning rash over Olive's skin.

"That reminds me," she said, pulling an empty lunch container out of her bag and pressing it into Rutherford's hands. "Please tell Mrs. Dewey thanks again for making all my lunches. And my dinners. Walter tried to fix dinner two days ago, and somehow he set canned soup on fire."

"I will relay the message," Rutherford announced. "Good luck with tonight's endeavors."

"Thanks," said Olive, opening the door. "See you tomorrow." With a last little wave at Rutherford, she stepped inside and locked the door behind her.

Walter's head popped through the library doors. "Hello, Olive," he rumbled.

"Hi, Walter," said Olive, hoping the distrust that prickled on her skin wouldn't seep into her voice.

"Mmm." Walter blinked at her. "How was your day?"

"It was fine." Olive dropped her book bag and leaned against the front door. "How was yours?"

"Excellent." Walter nodded, his head bobbing on his long, skinny neck, which in his black turtleneck looked even longer and skinnier. "No sign of trouble. And Horatio finally stopped ignoring me. When I said 'Good morning, Horatio,' he said 'Hmph' instead of nothing."

Olive forced a smile. "That's good."

"Mmm. I was wondering—um . . ." Walter hesitated. ". . . do you know—did the McMartins keep books anywhere besides the library? Maybe in the attic, or . . ."

"I don't think so," said Olive firmly. "Why?"

"I just—mmm—it seems strange that there isn't a single book about magic. Not in the whole library." Walter's voice grew even deeper as he drew his head toward his shoulders. "No magical history. Or folklore. Or anything."

Olive stared hard at Walter. He still reminded her of a giant bird. But now, in his black turtleneck, he looked less like a crane and more like a vulture.

"Maybe Ms. McMartin destroyed them," she said pointedly. "Maybe she didn't want *anyone else* to find them."

Walter's head bobbed in a way that might have been a nod.

"Well," Olive resumed, "I'm going up to my room for a while."

Olive started up the staircase. She looked back over her shoulder, just once, to see if Walter was watching her—but he had already vanished behind the closing wooden doors of the library.

Once she'd heard the doors click shut, Olive tugged the spectacles out of her collar. She raced the rest of the way up the stairs and dove into the painting of Linden Street.

In front of his tall gray house, Morton was hopping through the squares of a game of hopscotch. The chalk lines were rapidly disappearing from the pavement, and the acorn cap he threw flew straight back to its spot by his feet. He didn't look up as Olive approached.

"Can I play?" she asked.

Morton shrugged, stopping to pick up a stick of chalk and redraw the fading lines. "I don't know. That's up to Elmer." He nodded toward an empty spot on the sidewalk.

Olive had met Morton's invisible friends before. They weren't exactly *imaginary* friends. They had been real once, just like Morton—but unlike Morton, they had gone on being real. By now, they had probably grown up and gone away, while Morton never would.

She waved at the empty sidewalk. "That's okay, Elmer," she said. "But after you're done, maybe you could help me. Both of you."

"With what?" asked Morton, tossing the acorn cap. It landed on square 8, then zipped back to its starting spot.

"I thought we might sneak out of the house—we can't let anyone see us, because I'm not supposed to go anywhere on my own—and search for my parents."

Morton frowned at the pavement, flicking the acorn cap with his toe. "What if we find them? Won't *she* be there too? With the Old Man?"

"He can't be there," said Olive. "He's still stuck in his portrait. Probably."

Morton folded his spindly arms. "And how come you'll let me out of the house to look for your parents, but not *mine?*" With a ripple of his long white nightshirt, Morton whirled around. "I don't know if I will help you," he said.

"Morton, please!" Olive called. But Morton strode toward the crest of the hill without looking back.

They hurried up the quiet street, Morton storming ahead, Olive scurrying after. On either side, sleepy houses towered over them, their curtained windows staring out like blinded eyes. A few candles burned on the other side of foggy panes, tiny flecks of warmth pressing against the night.

"Please, Morton," Olive panted to the back of Morton's tufty head. "I don't know what to do. I don't know how to get either of our parents back. I'm just— I'm just trying to do the best I can."

Morton's footsteps began to slow. He didn't turn around, but he didn't move away as Olive caught up with him either. Side by side, they walked past a porch where a budding rosebush that would never bloom twined its thorny arms through the railings.

"I've never walked down this part of the street before," said Olive as they passed another deserted lawn.

"These houses are empty, mostly," said Morton.

Olive looked up at the dark windows and looming rooftops, enclosing spare rooms for guests who would never arrive—or, if they did, who would never leave again.

They passed a house with a rounded tower, its siding such a deep shade of green that in the twilight it looked almost black. The house might have vanished into the darkness, if not for a delicate light glowing in the first-floor windows of the tower. The light glimmered softly, like a candle, but it had a very un-candle-like color. This light was an unearthly greenish blue, like an aquamarine held in front of a fire.

Olive stopped, putting a hand on Morton's arm. "Who lives in that house?" she asked.

"In there?" Morton frowned up at the glowing windows. "No one."

Something feathery and nervous fluttered inside Olive's chest. "But there's a candle burning inside. Why would an empty house have a burning candle?"

Morton shrugged. "It's always been there." Slowly, he turned to follow the worn brick path that led to the stoop. Olive trailed after him. Their footsteps thudded on the wooden stairs.

They stood before the closed front door, wavering on their feet. At last, Olive reached up and tapped cautiously on the cold wood. There was no answer. Olive counted to ten under her breath ("You skipped *eight*," said Morton), but no one came. When she grasped the heavy brass knob and pushed the door inward, it pushed back at her. "Go inside, quick," Olive whispered. They darted across the threshold before the painted door could pull itself shut.

The slam echoed through the empty house. Keeping close to the door, Olive glanced around. No rugs lay on the floor. No lights hung from the ceilings. The walls were drab and bare. One lonely velvet couch sat in the front room, with no one sitting on it. The only light inside the house came from just around the corner, where the bluish glow reached toward them, beckoning them on.

Olive edged around the wall. Morton tiptoed behind her.

In the center of the bare, round room, there stood a small wooden table. Atop the small wooden table was a candle in a silver holder. Its flame danced lightly in Olive's breath as she leaned in, studying the wax's strange blue color, and the silvery coating that glittered atop it, almost like frost on a windowpane.

Olive gave a little gasp.

"It's a Calling Candle," she whispered.

"A Calling Candle?" Morton whispered back.

Olive's mind flew back along the painted street, where candles burned in window after window.

"Maybe they're *all* Calling Candles. Aldous could have used them to bring people in here."

Morton kept quiet.

Olive stared at the candle's bright flame. "But no one's in this house. I wonder if Aldous left the candle here, waiting for the next person, and just never used it. And if he never used it . . . that means that we *could*." Olive felt her heart jump higher and harder, like a huge metal pinball bouncing between her ribs. "We could call my parents."

Morton looked into Olive's eyes. "Or *my* parents," he said.

"Or Annabelle," Olive added as the pinball turned to a lump of ice.

Morton gave a little jerk. Instinctively, he put the hand that Annabelle had sliced with a dagger behind his back.

"It might be the safest thing to do," said Olive softly. "That way, at least she'd be stuck Elsewhere again."

For several silent moments, both Olive and Morton stared at the candle, like two starving people studying their last crumb of food.

Olive licked her papery lips. "So," she whispered. "Who should we call?"

"No one," said a sharp voice from behind them.

14

OLIVE AND MORTON whirled around.

Three pairs of bright green eyes glittered in the light of the candle.

"You should call no one," Horatio repeated, "because you haven't the faintest idea what you're doing."

"Where have you been?" Olive burst out as a confusing mixture of gladness and frustration rushed through her. "I've hardly seen you all week, and now you show up just in time to keep me from finally doing something worthwhile?"

"As it happens, Olive," said Horatio, fluffing his thick fur, "we have been doing something *worthwhile* too: Guarding this house's secrets and keeping you from making any dangerous mistakes. Apparently we are indeed 'just in time.'"

"But I haven't done anything," Olive protested. "*Nobody* has. My parents are gone, and it's been a whole week, and I can't keep wasting time!"

Leopold tilted his sleek black head. "Aren't Mrs. Dewey and Doctor Widdecombe and Walter's aunt Deluda—"

"Delora," Horatio corrected, "though 'Deluda' might be more appropriate."

"—aren't they making any progress?" Leopold finished.

"No." Olive spread her arms, exasperated. She looked back at the candle burning on the table. "And here I have the chance to do something real."

"No you don't, Olive," said Horatio. "And not merely because you *shouldn't* try to use an object as powerful as a Calling Candle, but because you don't know how."

"Yes I do!" Olive argued. "You hold the candle, and you say someone's name into the flames, and you can only use it once."

"As usual, Olive, you have approximately half of the necessary information," Horatio said dryly. "First, you can only call *one* person, so summoning *two* parents will pose a bit of a problem. Second, if the person you call is being held by other magic—under the influence of another spell, or trapped in another painting, perhaps—they cannot appear. Calling your parents could be a waste of time as well as a waste of a candle."

"Third," Harvey added, in a British accent, "you'd need the assistance of a fellow agent to keep the entrance open, in order for your target to be transported Elsewhere."

"What does that mean?" Olive asked.

"To put it in civilian terms: One of us would have to sit in the picture frame."

"Oh," said Olive. She gazed around at the three cats, their glossy coats shimmering in the candlelight. "You know, Agent 1-800, it seems funny that you would do that to help Aldous McMartin trap his enemies, but you won't do it to trap your own."

The cats were silent for a moment as the meaning of Olive's words sank in. Leopold cocked his head. Horatio's eyes narrowed.

Harvey raised one eyebrow. He turned slowly to the other cats. "I believe she has a point," he murmured.

"Olive," said Horatio in a low, measured voice, "think very carefully about the risks you run by bringing Annabelle McMartin here."

Morton took a step backward, pressing himself to the wall.

Olive pictured the painted Annabelle strolling gracefully up Morton's street. Her face would be cool and pretty and calm, and her eyes would be terrifying gold glints in the darkness. She would glide toward the porches, the hushed and frightened houses, the windows where Morton's neighbors stared out, cowering—

No. They would need to bring Annabelle someplace secure. Someplace where she couldn't hurt anyone else.

And Olive knew the perfect spot.

"I wouldn't call her here," Olive told Morton and the cats. "I'd call her into her own portrait. If she doesn't tell us everything we want to know, then we'll leave her there. She'll be stuck, just like she was before."

There was a moment of quiet as the three cats studied Olive, their shadows quivering on the wall.

"A clever plan, miss," said Leopold at last.

Horatio whirled toward him.

Leopold looked into Horatio's wide eyes. "Why not contain her, before she can plot any further harm to us?"

"Because 'containing' Annabelle in this house is like tossing a viper into your own bathtub," Horatio retorted.

"But Agent Olive's strategy could work," Harvey chimed in. "We may need to strike pretentiously in order to avoid a greater risk."

"He means *preemptively*," Leopold murmured to Olive. "A preemptive strike *is* generally wiser than an emptive one."

Horatio let out a sigh. "As all of you seem to agree,

and as I know how stubborn some of you are," he added, his eyes flicking to Olive, "I won't waste my time trying to dissuade you." With a flourish of his tail, the orange cat trotted toward the door.

"Are you leaving us, Horatio?" Olive asked, disappointed.

"I'm heading to Annabelle's portrait," Horatio snapped. "Allowing you to rush into this confrontation without a single sane witness seems like a bad idea."

Olive gave Horatio's receding tail a smile. Carefully, gently, she slipped her fingers through the metal loop of the candleholder and lifted it from the table. The candle's blue light flickered, but it didn't dim.

Morton held the front door of the house open as everyone else hurried out.

"I'm not coming with you," he muttered to Olive as the door thumped shut behind them. "You talk about magic too much. And it's not safe. And I don't . . ." Morton hesitated, twisting his bare toes against the floorboards. ". . . I don't want to see *her*."

Morton wouldn't meet her eyes, but Olive knew he was thinking of the last time they had confronted Annabelle together—when Lucinda had thrown herself between Morton and Annabelle, saving Morton from Annabelle's burst of fire by being burned herself.

"I understand," she said softly. She gave Morton's

arm an awkward pat before following the cats into the street.

Halfway down the hillside, Olive glanced over her shoulder. Morton stood at the crest of Linden Street, staring after them. The hem of his too-long white nightshirt rippled over his bare toes. "Be careful!" he called.

Olive gave him the bravest wave she could manage. She guessed this was what knights must have felt as they rode into combat: a mixture of anxiety and readiness and anger, all pushing down the fear that kept threatening to rise. Holding the candle steady before her, she hurried the rest of the way down the hill.

The upstairs hall was silent.

Horatio led the way along the corridor. Olive followed, flanked by the other two cats, keeping her eyes on the candle. Even in the late-afternoon light that floated through the house's windows, the glow of the candle was strangely vivid, its color unearthly, too startling to be beautiful. Olive cupped her hand around the flame, trying to keep any stray beams from flickering down the stairs and catching Walter's eye.

Inside the lavender bedroom, everyone paused. The cats sniffed the air. Olive wondered what their noses noticed, besides the scent of lilies of the valley and un-breathed air and emptiness. Olive shivered.

Harvey leaped onto the chest of drawers below the picture frame. "Begin Operation Tea Party Two," he announced into his imaginary transistor wristwatch.

"When did we decide on that name?" asked Leopold, stiffening to his most commanding height. "I believe we ought to call this the Lavender Battle."

"The Lavender Battle?" Harvey repeated, looking dubious.

"Perhaps you've heard of the War of the Roses," said Leopold, even more stiffly.

"What do you say, Agent Orange?" Harvey asked. "Operation Tea Party Two or the Lavender Battle?"

Horatio rolled his eyes. "Why not call it 'Art Restoration' and get it over with?"

"Operation Art Restoration," said Harvey. "I like it." He slipped through the frame, with Leopold marching after.

Horatio waited until Olive had clambered up onto the chest of drawers before following the others into the painting. She adjusted the spectacles with one hand, made sure the candle was steady in the other, and dragged herself backward through the frame with one arm in the air, like someone heading down a playground slide while holding an ice-cream cone.

She landed on her knees on a slippery silk couch, still holding the candle over her head. She flipped around, surveying the painted room. Everything looked exactly as it had on her first visit. Unwilting bunches of lilies and lilacs clustered in porcelain vases. Polished seashells and figurines decorated each surface. The cats had already darted off in three directions, peering under furnishings, checking each corner, sniffing at the fireless fireplace. Olive pulled herself out of the sofa cushions and ventured toward the tea table.

The silver filigree teapot still sat where Annabelle had left it. Two cups and saucers waited on the spotless tablecloth, flanked by delicate silver spoons. Olive set the candle down in the center of the table before picking up the cup that she had sipped from months ago, on her first visit with Annabelle. The cup was still warm. Olive picked a sugar cube from the bowl and plopped it into the cup. She took a tiny, tentative sip. The tea was still not sweet enough—maybe because the sugar cube Olive had just dropped in had appeared again, whole and dry, inside the sugar bowl.

With a deep breath, Olive set the cup back in its place and picked up the Calling Candle. "Is everybody ready?" she asked, wondering why she felt compelled to whisper. "Should we start?"

"The area is clear," said Harvey, in Agent 1-800's British accent. "I will monitor the entrance." He bounced up from the back of the couch and perched on the bottom of the frame, his body half inside, half outside the painting.

"Remember to keep your distance from her," Horatio warned, moving toward Olive. "Don't let her come near enough to touch the spectacles. And remember to *think* before you speak."

"I will."

"If she turns violent, we will defend you," Leopold said, in his gruffest voice. "You can be sure of that."

Olive gave him a shaky smile. "Thank you, Leopold."

She took another breath. Now that she was about to do it, bringing Annabelle here felt almost insane—just like dropping a viper into your bubble bath, as Horatio had said, or lowering a spider down your own shirt collar. But she had come this far, and she couldn't go back—not if she wanted to see her parents again.

"Okay," she whispered, more to herself than to the cats. She raised the candle with both hands. Its flame was tinted and transparent at the same time, like a droplet of molten glass. Olive stared into the layers of burning color, from the purplish halo around the wick to the ripples of aquamarine and emerald that paled to gold-white at the top.

"*Annabelle McMartin.*" The flame shivered in her breath. "*Annabelle McMartin. Annabelle McMartin.*"

The candlelight began to pulse. A sudden breeze entered the room, fluttering the lace curtains, making the tablecloth billow and the teacups rattle. Olive felt the air swirl around her, an invisible wave flooding the room. The back of her neck prickled sharply. In her hand, the candle dimmed, its flame shrinking to a crumb of turquoise fire.

Then, as suddenly as if someone had flicked a switch, the wind died. The tablecloth straightened itself. The curtains rippled into place. The flames of the candle brightened again, only now they were the yellow-gold flames of any ordinary candle—like all the other candles inside the painted windows of Linden Street.

And standing inside the parlor, with waves of smooth dark hair and a string of pearls gleaming softly around her neck, was a young woman in a long white dress.

15

THE PRICKLE IN Olive's neck flooded down her spine, collecting in an icy pool in the pit of her stomach. The candle trembled in her hands. Leopold and Horatio pressed steadyingly against her legs. Harvey jumped down from the picture frame and planted himself beside the other cats, glaring up.

"Well, Olive Dunwoody," said Annabelle, in a voice like poisoned sugar. "Are you playing with magic again?" She stepped closer to Olive, and the candlelight cast its rippling sheen over her painted skin. Her golden eyes glimmered. "You'd better be careful, or you'll burn your fingers."

Olive took a small step backward, clutching the candle protectively in front of her body, and bumped into the squishy couch. The cats stayed as stony and silent as sculptures. "You're trying to scare me," she said, hoping she sounded less terrified than she felt. "But you can't hurt us here. This whole house is surrounded by protective spells, and we have allies all over Linden Street, keeping watch."

"This is *Elsewhere,* Olive," said Annabelle. Her painted mouth formed a tiny smile. "Your neighbors can't save you here."

"Y-yes they can," Olive stammered. "If you try anything, one of the cats will run for help. Rutherford will know that we need him before a message could get there anyway. Besides, now that Aldous is gone—from this house, I mean—you don't have any power here. Not anymore."

"We'll see," said Annabelle, her smile unwavering. She leaned down, bringing her face close to Olive's. The pools of paint in her eyes were flat and cold. Olive swallowed. With a delicate puff, Annabelle blew the candle out. "First things first," she said, in her sweetest kindergarten-teacher voice. "Why don't you tell me what you think you're doing by calling me here?"

Olive set the snuffed candle on the tea table, nearly knocking it over with her rubbery hands. "You have something I want," she said, trying to keep her voice steady. "And if you don't help me get it, we'll leave you stuck in here. Just like you were before."

"Is that so?" Annabelle looked mildly amused. "And

just what would I need to do to escape this *terrifying* threat?"

"You—you need—" Olive faltered, staring at the gold in Annabelle's painted eyes. "If you don't want us to trap you here forever, you'll have to give me my parents back."

A strange expression flickered across Annabelle's face, but it was gone again before Olive had the chance to identify it. "Two prisoners in exchange for one?" she asked. "That doesn't sound like a fair exchange. In fact, I think it's only fair that you lost your parents in the first place." Her rosebud mouth snaked into a smile. "You removed my family from our home, and now we have removed yours."

Olive glanced down at the cats, standing steady and silent around her. "It's *our* home now," she said. "And you haven't removed *me*."

"This house will never belong to you," said Annabelle, as if Olive hadn't spoken at all. "But as long as we are bargaining, why don't we make it an even exchange?" She paused for a moment, tapping one finger thoughtfully against her chin. "Shall we say a pair of parents for a pair of spectacles?"

Olive sucked in a breath. "No!"

"Very well." Annabelle gave a dainty shrug. "If you refuse to compromise, I won't tell you anything at all."

Olive looked down at the cats again. They kept

quiet. "But . . . then you would be stuck here," she said hesitantly.

"Is that what you really want, Olive?" Annabelle's smile widened. "You want me back inside of this house, with all of your friends?" Her eyes flicked to the cats, glimmering. "Really, that's quite generous of you. I would be much closer to what I want. And you would be no closer to what *you* want." Annabelle gave a little toss of her head. "It's your choice, I suppose. If you don't really want to learn what I know about your parents . . ."

"Wait," said Olive, more urgently than she meant to. "You mean . . . if I *do* give you the spectacles, you would tell me exactly where my parents are?"

The cats' eyes, six burning arrows, zoomed from Olive's face to Annabelle's.

"I think that's fair," said Annabelle. She bent down again, bringing her eyes in line with Olive's. She dropped her voice to a compassionate murmur. "I'm sure that waiting and wondering about them has been terrible, hasn't it, Olive?" Olive looked down, away from Annabelle, fighting the prickling pressure in her eyes. Annabelle's gentle voice went on. "You just want to know if they are *alive*—if they are safe, if they are scared, if they are in pain. If there is any way you can put your family together again. Don't you?" She waited. Olive pinched her tongue between her teeth, fighting the urge to answer. "I know you do," Annabelle breathed. "So you will give me the spectacles, and in exchange, I will tell you everything I know about where to find your parents."

Olive tugged the spectacles off her nose. They fell, caught by their ribbon, and bumped softly against her chest. "Wait . . ." she said again. "You'll know that I'm handing you the spectacles. But how will I know that you're telling me the truth?"

"An excellent question, Olive," said Horatio, speaking up at last.

Annabelle ignored the cat. She arched her delicate eyebrows. "As it happens, I *was* going to tell you the truth, Olive. But if you like, why don't I swear on something we both love?" She glanced around the painted room, her eyes sweeping coldly over the cats, gliding across the silk couch, the lacy windows, the row of photographs along the mantelpiece. "I swear by my house," she said. "My beautiful house, which sheltered my family for generations, and which will continue to shelter us until its stones dissolve into sand—that I will tell you everything I know."

Olive swallowed. Her trembling fingers reached to pull the spectacles' ribbon from around her neck. Before she could tug it over her head, a black shape streaked in front of her.

"No, miss," said Leopold. "We cannot let the spectacles fall into her possession."

"But I need to know where my—"

"I understand, miss." Leopold paused. "And that is why I will offer myself in their place."

Horatio froze. Harvey made a small, startled noise.

Olive felt the breath whoosh out of her lungs. "Leopold, *no.*"

"It will be safer this way." Leopold turned to face Annabelle, raising his head and puffing out his glossy black chest.

Annabelle's eyes fastened on Leopold like two golden hooks. "You willingly enter my service?"

"I do," the cat answered.

With the heel of her shoe, Annabelle scratched a line across the parlor's pastel rug. Looking more than ever like a miniature panther, Leopold squared his shoulders, stepped over the already fading line, and seated himself at Annabelle's side. His eyes met Olive's for a fraction of a second, and then shifted away, staring with soldierly steadiness into the distance.

Olive had stopped breathing. She didn't realize this until her chest began to ache and the room tilted dizzily to one side, like an egg sliding out of a greased pan. She swallowed a mouthful of air.

"And now," said Annabelle, leaning closer to Olive's gaping face, "I will tell you everything I know about where to find your parents." She paused, letting the moment stretch.

Olive's heart thumped against her shriveling lungs.

"I know *nothing*," Annabelle said sweetly. "I do not know where they are. I don't know where you'll find them . . . if you can find them at all. You see, *I* am not fighting alone either. And you cannot get rid of my family, Olive. Not as long as you infest our home like the little pest that you are." Annabelle straightened, smiling again. "Now, this is what I would call 'fair.' I reclaim a bit of what was already mine. You learn a bit of the truth."

The shock and rage that shot through Olive were so thick, so heavy, that she couldn't move. She could only stand and stare as Annabelle bent down and swept Leopold into her arms, holding the huge black cat securely against her chest. Leopold kept completely still. He did not look at Olive or anyone else.

"Good night, everyone," said Annabelle. Then she stepped onto the sofa and climbed gracefully through the frame. There was a muted creak from the lavender room's door, and she and Leopold were gone.

Olive managed to take a breath at last. It came back out in a roar. "We have to get him back!" she shouted, whirling to face the cats.

Harvey merely stared at her. When Horatio spoke, his voice was soft and hollow. "And how will we do that, Olive?" he asked. "With Leopold in her possession, Annabelle can come and go freely; she can leave

or enter any painting . . ." Horatio stopped. His last words hung in the air, like smoke from a distant and terrible fire.

"This wasn't how it was supposed to go!" Olive cried, digging her fingernails into her palms. "We were controlling *her* for once! I thought—if we just gave her the spectacles, we might—"

"No. Leopold was right," Horatio cut her off. "With the spectacles, Annabelle would have been far more dangerous. Leopold has a will of his own. He may be able to resist her commands, and delay setting Aldous free." Horatio hesitated. "For a while."

"No." Olive clenched her fists even harder. If she hadn't known it would just pick itself up again, she would have kicked over the elegant little tea table, sending its china and silver smashing through the air. She wanted to destroy something that would last. "No," she said again. "They can't keep controlling us! *This isn't their house!*"

Shoving the spectacles back onto her face, Olive leaped for the couch. She tumbled through the frame, banging her forehead on the chest of drawers and somersaulting onto the carpet. The door of the lavender room stood open.

Olive shot into the hall, but there was no trace of Leopold and Annabelle. The glimmering paintings, the dusty carpets, the heavy wooden doors sealing off the empty bedrooms all seemed to be watching her. Sneering at her. Annabelle's words echoed inside her head: *This house will never belong to you . . .*

Olive let out a furious breath. She pictured a wrecking ball smashing through the ancient walls, the stones tumbling down like a stack of toppled blocks. She imagined fire sweeping through the detritus, consuming every shred of what was left: the curtains, the carpets, the canvases on the walls, all of the McMartins' things crumbling into ash, and then into nothing.

Scowling at the floor beneath her feet, Olive thundered down the stairs, running straight into the coatrack in a turtleneck that was climbing in the opposite direction.

"Olive," rumbled Walter, "what was—"

"Walter!" Olive grabbed his baggy sleeve. "I need to talk to your aunt and uncle," she panted, tightening her grip. "I need to talk to them *now*."

Since Halloween night, the Nivenses' dining room had grown to look even less like a place to eat and even more like a mortician's garage sale. On the sideboard, a bouquet of dead roses lay near a rusty handsaw. Several small, sharp tools, of the sort you might find in a dentist's office, were arranged in the center of the table, next to a glossy black feather far too long to have come from any raven on earth.

Doctor Widdecombe paced slowly along the length of the room. Walter had settled on the sideboard, his bulbous eyes fixed on Olive. Delora sat very still at one end of the table, staring into the distance, with her mirror positioned before her. Olive sat—not very still at all—at the other end. She fumed in her chair, both knees bouncing with angry impatience. The words of her explanation seemed to hang in the air above them, like foul-smelling smoke.

"So, in spite of all of our advice, you summoned the portrait of Annabelle McMartin into the house," said Doctor Widdecombe, whisking a jar filled with small, dirty cotton balls off of the end of the table. "Rolled cobwebs," he explained peripherally. "They have powerful sleep-inducing properties." He set the jar on a shelf, next to what looked like a giant hairball on a silver platter. "She took one of the familiars and escaped, once again. Is that correct?"

"I—I just couldn't wait anymore," Olive stammered, clenching her hands in her lap. Her skin prickled with a mixture of embarrassment and rage. "And it didn't even matter. Annabelle doesn't know where my parents are."

"How do you know she doesn't?" Delora asked softly. Her eyes fixed on something several feet above Olive's head.

"Because—because she said so," Olive answered, glancing up at the empty air.

"Didn't you think she might have been lying to you?"

"She swore she wasn't," said Olive, her cheeks burning with a fresh wave of heat. "She swore on her family's house that she was telling the truth."

Doctor Widdecombe and Delora exchanged a look.

Doctor Widdecombe paused in his pacing. "This *is* a dangerous turn of events," he said. "The fact that she has one of the familiars—a living key to Elsewhere—changes everything about our own plans."

"I know." Olive swallowed. She looked from Delora's wide silvery eyes to Doctor Widdecombe's crinkly hazel ones. "And it's my fault. But I'll do anything to fix it, and to get rid of the McMartins for good. *Anything.*"

Doctor Widdecombe resumed his pacing. Light from the oil lamps flickered over his snug tweed jacket.

"As you heard Mrs. Dewey say, Olive," he began, "the process that Delora and I suggested is directly opposed to the work that we, as members of the S.M.U.D.S., intend to do. She was right to discourage it."

Olive felt her heart plummet to the base of her stomach and smash like a slushy snowball.

"It is true that this may be the only course—the *only* course," Doctor Widdecombe repeated, with extra emphasis, "that would remove the power of the McMartins' legacy from the house once and for all—but it requires dangerous magic. Is it worth it, one might ask, to fight evil with evil, darkness with darkness?"

"Mmm—I think—" Walter began timidly.

"This is what we, as powerful magicians, must ask ourselves," Doctor Widdecombe plowed on, sweeping one hand toward Delora and the other toward his own straining coat buttons. Walter bowed his head.

"Byron," murmured Delora. She leaned over the mirror, bending closer and closer until Olive thought she might fall straight into it. "I believe I can see the answer."

Olive sat higher in her chair, craning over the table. All she could see in the mirror was the reflection of Delora's own empty gray eyes.

"What is it, Aunt Delora?" Walter asked.

"Yes," Delora breathed. "The answer is *yes.*"

In a tight line, laden with two big black bags, Delora, Doctor Widdecombe, Olive, and Walter slunk through the thinnest part of the lilac hedge and headed toward the back door of the old stone house. Above them, the sky paled with the last purple hues of sunset.

"Couldn't I help? Or even—um—just watch?" Walter's rumbling voice carried through the dimness.

"You *will* be helping, Walter," said Doctor Widdecombe, shoving a lilac branch out of his wide way. "Distracting the remaining familiars is absolutely vital to our success."

They stepped onto the back porch, leaving Walter standing dejectedly in the yard.

"Once you've gotten them out of the house, you can guard the front door," Doctor Widdecombe added.

"Don't let anyone disturb us—especially Lydia Dewey. And remember that the rest of the house must be kept in perfect darkness. Don't get frightened and turn on any lights."

Walter nodded, but he kept silent.

He was still staring after them when Olive turned back to close the door, and something in his expression made Olive think of a huge, hook-beaked raptor about to swoop down on its prey. But then Walter turned, shuffling off across the twilit lawn, and he looked like a gangly water bird once again.

As she and Doctor Widdecombe and Delora hurried through the kitchen, switching off all the lights as they went, Olive heard a soft rattle, like a handful of pebbles hitting the glass of an upstairs window. Walter was causing the first distraction; at any moment, the cats would come rushing downstairs to see what had caused the sound, and Olive, Delora, and Doctor Widdecombe would be deep in the darkness of the basement, with the door closed securely behind them.

Olive stopped at the bottom of the creaking basement stairs, shivering slightly. The soft murmurs of Doctor Widdecombe and Delora drifted in the blackness before her. She heard scrapes and thumps and glassy tinkles, and then the sound of a match being struck, and one small, guttering flame burst out of the darkness several feet away. The flame split into two, and then split again, until Olive could make out Delora's black-draped form in the center of a burning ring of candles.

Olive glanced into the basement's darkest corner, where a pair of green eyes should have been reflecting the candlelight. Now there was only darkness. She was making the right choice, Olive reassured herself. The *only* choice. Delora and Doctor Widdecombe knew what they were doing, and they would help her to get rid of the McMartins—*all* of the McMartins—before they could hurt anyone else.

"Olive." Delora beckoned her closer. "Come here."

Picking up her legs very high, because setting herself on fire would be one unpleasant problem too many, Olive hopped over the circle of candles and approached the spot where Delora stood.

A wide metal bowl waited at their feet. Olive watched as Delora poured a stream of liquid from a glass bottle into its base. "Now," said Delora, holding out a box of matches for Olive to take, "you must add the fire."

Something about this moment—the anticipation, the bowl waiting below her—made Olive think of the moment in the painted forest when Annabelle had spilled Morton's blood into the urn of Aldous's ashes. *But this is completely different,* Olive told herself. They were getting rid of something, not *creating* it. And these were her allies, not her enemies.

Her hands shook slightly, but Olive managed to light a match and drop it into the bowl. There was a muted *whump* as the liquid caught fire. Delora stepped back, tossing a handful of strange-colored leaves and twigs into the flames. Before long, billows of gray smoke filled the basement, nestling like another layer of cobwebs between the dusty rafters. Every few seconds, Delora leaned over the bowl and tossed in another herb. Her shadow bent and stretched toward the surrounding walls, flickering over the ancient gravestones.

"Not much longer now," said Doctor Widdecombe cheerily from outside the circle.

"You said this will destroy the root of the McMartins' power, right?" Olive asked, looking at him through the ring of candlelight.

Doctor Widdecombe's smiling features glowed back at her. "A spell's exact effects can be difficult to predict, but that is indeed the desired outcome."

"Olive, stay just where you are," said Delora, before stepping over the circle of candles and gliding toward the wall. With ash from a filigreed silver jar, she left a swipe along the edge of each gravestone. Doctor Widdecombe's eyes followed his wife, so full of happy anticipation that Delora might have been pulling cookies out of the oven instead of leaving fingerprints on long-dead witches' graves. The thought of cookies led Olive back to Mrs. Dewey, but the guilt she knew she should feel seemed far-off and unimportant now. They were doing what needed to be done. Experts like Doctor Widdecombe and Delora wouldn't steer her wrong.

When the last stone had been marked, Delora drifted toward the foot of the stairs and stopped at Doctor Widdecombe's side. "Place your hands over the bowl, Olive," she instructed.

Olive obeyed. The heat of the fire pressed up against her palms.

"You must concentrate as you cast the spell. Now, repeat after me—"

"Wait," said Olive. "*Me?* But I'm not magical. I don't—"

"We are well aware of your limitations, Olive," said Doctor Widdecombe, with an encouraging smile. "You are only a conduit. A conductor of messages, as it were."

"Isn't Delora the one who's supposed to be a messenger?" Olive asked, wavering. Her hands twitched nervously above the burning bowl.

"This house knows you. Its powers recognize you," said Delora.

Olive glanced warily at the walls. She *did* have the

feeling that each stone was watching her. She'd had that feeling ever since her family had moved in.

"Those on the other side will obey *you*, not me." Delora's voice was soft and calming. "It's very simple," she added. "You must only keep still, and repeat my words."

You're the one who suggested this, Olive told herself. *Don't you want to get rid of the McMartins' powers for good? Won't you at least* try?

". . . Okay," Olive whispered.

Delora spoke slowly, making sure that Olive caught every word. "I call you from earth. From stone. From silence. From sleep."

The fire had faded to embers, but Olive could still feel its warmth against her palms. "Um . . . I call you from earth. From stone . . ." The back of her neck began to prickle. By glancing out of the corners of her eyes, she could tell that there was nothing to see—nothing but the basement's dimness, and the candlelight flickering over ash-smudged stones. "From silence. From sleep."

"I call you," Delora prompted, her soft voice rustling over the walls. "From dirt. From bone. To come forth. To obey."

The prickle on Olive's neck grew more insistent. "I call you from dirt. From bone. To come forth. To obey."

The fire in the bowl was burning out. But the air went on filling with something thick and dark—something too thick and dark to be smoke. From the gravestones behind the dryer, black, weightless streams were beginning to pour. Olive sneaked a glance over her shoulder. From the other gravestones—from the names of *Athdar* and *Aíllíl* and *Angus* and *Anna McMartin*—wisps of misty blackness rippled to the ground.

Olive's arms started to tremble.

The black wisps thickened, and the darkness poured faster, until it was gushing from the graves, rising, twisting, slithering through the room. Doctor Widdecombe and Delora took a step back as the darkness rippled past them. It encircled the spot where Olive stood, keeping just outside the ring of candlelight.

"What is that?" Olive whispered.

Doctor Widdecombe's voice came from somewhere beyond the pool of darkness. "That is all that is left of the McMartins."

"You mean—this is—like ghosts?" Olive squeaked as a dark coil flowed uncomfortably close to the circle of candles.

"Creatures like the McMartins don't have 'ghosts,'" Doctor Widdecombe's voice answered. "These are their shades. We see them now as they truly were."

The darkness pouring from the stones thinned to

a trickle, and then to a stop. Olive watched the last tumbling wisps flow to the center of the room, where a swamp of shadows, dense and drifting, pooled around the circle of light. Then, as Olive stared, the shadows began to split apart. Creatures with fins and tentacles and layered rows of teeth rose up amid the blackness. A spider the size of a pony picked its needle-thin legs out of the dark. Something that looked like a wolf, but with legs two times too long, licked its muzzle with a black tongue. Olive's mind leaped back to the night when she'd faced what was no longer Aldous McMartin, but something made of his portrait, and his ashes, and Morton's not-quite-blood. On that night, darkness had filled the entire house, concealing hosts of slithering, hissing things that had dragged their icy touch over her skin. A sick feeling—like the moment just after you lose your balance, but before your body hits the ground—washed through her.

Delora's voice was repeating something that Olive couldn't quite hear. Her heartbeat rumbled in her ears.

The crawling, lumbering, slithering darkness moved inward, toward the circle of light. Olive could make out dragging, leathery wings, an angler fish's gaping jaws. The light of the candles fluttered over them, momentarily erasing bits of their black bodies, which faded and returned as the light slipped away.

Olive blinked, looking harder. No, the light didn't

cause the shades to disappear. Instead, as it touched them, it revealed human faces—actual human faces and actual human bodies, as faint and pale as the shapes formed by rising smoke. They were the faces of men and women, with craggy features and dark, deep-set eyes. McMartin faces. And the faces themselves were changing, shifting from young to old, old to young, floating through entire lifetimes within a few seconds. But the fire in the bowl had burned out, and the light of the candles was weak. The darkness was larger, and much, much stronger.

"I call you." Delora was shouting now. "And *I cast you out.*"

Olive's voice stuck in her throat. "I—I call you . . ." she choked. ". . . And I cast you out."

The words died away, leaving the basement so quiet that Olive could hear the candles sputtering.

One of the smoky silhouettes—one with a long, reptilian body—started to laugh. It was a strange sound, more like water steaming in a huge iron kettle than real laughter, but Olive knew that laughter was what it was. Another of the shades joined in, and then another and another.

In the center of the circle, Olive wobbled on her feet. "Is it working?" she called through the shifting ring of shadows. If Delora gave an answer, Olive couldn't hear it.

Olive took a deep, freezing breath. *"I cast you out!"* she shouted.

Her voice ricocheted from the walls.

The shades fell silent.

Then, as one, they rushed inward, silhouettes paling and warping in the light. Olive felt a wave of freezing air sweep over her, blowing out all but three of the candles. She heard Delora gasp. In the dimness, a giant, bony dog lumbered forward. Olive watched its toothy muzzle dissolve into a woman's smile as it bent toward the flames. There was a soft, whooshing sound, and the last of the light was gone.

In the darkness, Doctor Widdecombe let out a shriek that shook the dust from the rafters. With an audible rip from his tweed jacket, he dove for the staircase.

"Run, Byron!" Delora cried. Olive heard her steps creaking up the stairs after him.

"Wait!" Olive screamed. She plunged forward, knocking over the metal bowl. Dead candles clattered and rolled around her feet. A frigid wall of air broke over her, slippery fingers and claws and hands dragging at her skin, and then she was scrabbling on all fours up the rickety wooden staircase. The icy nearness of the shades rushed just behind her. Eely tendrils grasped at her ankles.

Doctor Widdecombe, Delora, and Olive raced

through the basement door into the kitchen. With all the lights off and evening settling outside, only the streetlamps and a sliver of moon saved the house from total darkness. Olive slammed the basement door shut behind her, but a black trail, slick and smooth as spilled oil, poured instantly from beneath it, looming back into hideous forms once it had snaked free.

"We can't stop them!" Delora shouted, glancing over her shoulder. Her hand locked around Olive's wrist. "Just *run!*"

Dragging Olive behind her, Delora flew through the kitchen and into the hall, with Doctor Widdecombe chuffing ahead of them like a tweed train engine.

Walter stood at the end of the hallway, gazing out the windows near the front door. Olive watched his face swivel toward them in the dimness. "I had to set a little fire near the porch to keep the familiars occupied," he began, "but—"

Walter's lanky body stiffened. His gaze traveled away from his aunt and uncle toward the wave of monstrous shadows rushing down the hall behind them.

"Open the door!" Doctor Widdecombe roared.

Walter fumbled at the knob. He managed to yank the door open just in time for Doctor Widdecombe to bolt *through* rather than *into* it. The professor's hefty frame bounded off the porch steps and puffed away into the night.

"Run, Walter!" Delora panted. "Get out! Escape this cursed place!"

Walter hesitated. His wide eyes flicked from Delora to Olive to the throng of approaching shadows. "Mmm—but I'm supposed to—" he began.

"Run!" Delora screamed.

Walter paused for another fraction of a second, his Adam's apple bobbing. Then he too rushed through the door and disappeared into the darkness.

Delora hurtled after him, still yanking Olive by the arm. Something long and boneless, like the limb of a giant squid, lashed over the floor beneath their feet. Icy fingers coiled around Olive's leg. The front door gaped before them. In three more steps, they would be outside, running away into the night—

—abandoning the house to the McMartin family.

"Wait!" Olive shouted. She locked her knees, skidding over the slippery floorboards as Delora dragged her forward. "We can't just run away!"

"Olive, you cannot stay here!" Delora insisted, yanking her toward the door.

Part of Olive—the larger, louder part—wanted to dive straight through that open doorway, to run to the safety of the Nivens house, or to the even cozier safety of Mrs. Dewey's house just beyond. But another part of her—a deeper, quieter part—knew that if she left, the McMartins would have won. She'd be abandoning the house, and Elsewhere, and Morton, and the cats, wherever they were. She would be fleeing from her own mistakes, leaving her friends to live with their terrible consequences.

She could stay and try to save them, or she could run away and save herself.

Lunging sideways, Olive hooked her arms through the banister that led up the staircase. "I won't leave!" she shouted, holding on tight as the skittering, lumbering forms moved closer. The darkness thickened, the chill of the shades' presence washing through the air. "This is *our* house!"

Delora gave a desperate growl. With a shake of her head, she released Olive's wrist and dove for the doorway, slamming it firmly shut behind her—leaving Olive and the twisting mass of shadows sealed inside.

The air plunged from cold to frigid. Olive hugged the banister, shuddering. Even with her eyes squeezed almost shut, she could feel the shades pressing closer. She knew with perfect certainty that no one was coming to rescue her—not the cats, not the neighbors, and certainly not her parents. She was alone in the icy darkness, with the McMartins' furious dead.

She kept very still, her arms twined through the banister, as the shades trailed their insect legs and slippery tails over her skin. The last breath she'd managed to suck into her lungs prickled like shards of ice.

"Intruder . . ." whispered a voice in her ear—a voice so faint that at first it was drowned out by the echo of Olive's own heartbeat. *"Intruder . . ."*

"I'm not intruding," said Olive shakily. She wrapped her arms even tighter around the polished spokes of the banister. "My family *bought* this house. There were no more McMartins to live in it."

"Trespasser!" hissed a voice that crawled over the skin like a spider.

"I'm not *trespassing*," Olive said, as firmly as she could. "You've all died out. You're extinct. Like—like—" She groped for a term Rutherford would use. "Like iguanodons," she finished.

"Liar!" the voices growled. *"Liar!"*

Something with the legs of a giant centipede inched up the side of Olive's neck. The tip of one huge, hooked claw trailed down her arm. In spite of the darkness, Olive closed her eyes.

"Do ye know what our family does to intruders?" a voice breathed into her ear.

Without looking, Olive knew that the shades were closing in on her, their blackness seeping straight through her skin, freezing her lungs, chilling the blood that ran through her veins. Her heartbeat began to slow. When she took a breath, shards of ice prickled in her throat, and she wondered if she was inhaling the shades themselves.

She had felt this sort of cold before. She had felt it in the attic of the old stone house, where all that was left of Aldous McMartin—more than a shade; a monster of paint and ashes and no-longer-human blood—had tried to get rid of her. He had frightened her, and frozen her, and nearly convinced her to give in. But in the end, she had defeated *him*.

Olive took a deep, cold breath. "You can't do anything to me," she said. She jerked upright, tossing her head so that the crawling thing slipped away. With a lunge, she skidded across the dark hallway to the light switch.

In the sudden electric glow, the monstrous black forms faded to human outlines. Insect legs vanished. Toothy jaws disappeared. A cluster of gray faces followed her, sunken-eyed and angry, as Olive darted into the parlor and then to the dining room, turning on the next light and the next, until the whole hallway was glowing. She pressed her back against the wall's wood paneling, staring out at the figures that wavered before her.

"See?" she said, less shakily now. "You're just—" Olive paused, looking around at the shifting faces, their familiar, craggy features and deep-set eyes. "You're nothing," she said. "You're memories. You're *stains.*"

Glowering, silent, the shades backed away. Olive

watched them slither into the house's remaining dark places. They crawled under furniture, behind curtains, into corners, regaining their inhuman forms.

With her jaw set and her chin in the air, Olive strode around the rest of the first floor, hitting each light switch and turning the knob of each lamp. She could feel the shades watching her from their patches of darkness, but she wasn't going to let them see that she was afraid . . . not even when something with fingers a foot long reached out of the blackness beneath the old brown couch.

She had turned on each light in the kitchen and the family room and was heading for the huge brass chandelier that hung in the library, when something surprising caught her eye.

There was already a light coming from the library. She could see its reddish glow seeping through the crack in the doors. This light hadn't been glowing a few minutes ago, she was certain. And the light was accompanied by a soft crackling sound—a sound Olive had heard many times before, but never in this room. It was the sound of a fire burning in a fireplace.

Cautiously, Olive pushed open the library's double doors.

The room was dim. But inside the enormous fireplace, its glow dancing across the chipped tiles, there burned a small and cheerful fire. Seated before the fire, in one of the velvet chairs so old that its upholstery had worn away in small bald patches, was a very small, very old woman.

In spite of the fire, Olive felt a sudden chill.

The old woman looked up. Her hair was pure white, pinned into a high, soft bun, and she wore a neat gray skirt and sweater. A strand of pearls gleamed around her shriveled neck. Her skin was pale . . . No, not pale, but *misty,* smoky, changing. As Olive stared, the old woman's face smoothed and her stooped back straightened, revealing the cold, pretty features and thick, dark hair of Annabelle McMartin.

"Hello, Olive Dunwoody," she said as her hair faded to white once again. But the smile that Olive knew so well remained, sweet and icy, on her inhuman lips.

17

"Please sit down, Olive," said the shade of Annabelle McMartin, gesturing to a vacant velvet chair.

Like a sleepwalker, Olive obeyed. She shuffled across the huge, dim room and plunked down into the chair so hard that it sent up a cloud of dust.

"You—you're Ms. McMartin," she stammered.

The old woman gave Olive an elegant nod. "I am. But you may call me Annabelle."

"I'd rather not," said Olive.

Something black and many-jointed slid through the doorway and skulked into the shadows at the back of the room, where the firelight didn't reach.

"Doesn't my family frighten you?" Ms. McMartin asked, watching Olive with eyes as sharp as scalpels.

"They can't hurt me." Olive shivered as Ms. McMartin's face shifted yet again, revealing a flash of Annabelle's features. "*You* frighten me," she added, before she could stop herself.

Ms. McMartin smiled. It was not a comforting smile. "But I can't hurt you either, Olive. And I don't even intend to try."

"How come—" A log in the fire tumbled, sending a patch of black shadow sliding over Ms. McMartin's arm. It was gone again too quickly for Olive to see what form the darkness had revealed. "How come your voice is so much clearer than the others'?" she asked. "How come you *look* clearer?"

"Less time has passed for me than for them." Ms. McMartin turned back toward the crackling fire. "Things fade away eventually. Most things, that is."

Olive twitched in her chair. She glanced around the room, at the high rows of shelves, the dark slit of sky between the velvet curtains, the glimmering firelight on the dancing girls' frame. "So, if you're here now, like *this,* does that mean that you . . ." Olive wavered, remembering the gravestones and the urn of Aldous McMartin's ashes hidden below the basement. "Does that mean that *you* were buried here somewhere too?"

The smoky outline of Ms. McMartin shook her head. "My grandfather's wishes were not my wishes. But I *did* die in this room," she continued lightly. "I spent a great deal of time here. Of course, when you have lived in one house for over a century, you have spent a great deal of time *everywhere.*"

"I guess so," said Olive, lifting her feet off the carpet.

"I loved the front parlor as well," Ms. McMartin went on. "And the dining room. And my own bedroom, naturally."

Olive nodded. "I like the library and the family room. And the kitchen, especially on weekend mornings. And the porch. And the attic. I even kind of almost like the basement, because Leopold—" The name caught in Olive's throat.

"Ah yes. The cats," said Ms. McMartin, with an exasperated sigh. "What a change it must have been for them, having you move into this place."

Olive swallowed. Yes, she'd caused many changes for the cats, some probably for the better, and some definitely for the worse. She hoped that Harvey and Horatio had found someplace safe to hide during this latest change. She nodded again, unable to speak.

The flickering glow of the fire shone straight through Ms. McMartin's body, filtering through the skirt and sweater that rippled into one of Annabelle's long lacy gowns.

Olive chewed the inside of her cheek. "So, how . . ." she began. "How did you . . . um . . ."

"How did I *die?*" Ms. McMartin supplied impatiently. "You can say the word, Olive. I think we've passed the point of squeamishness."

Olive cleared her throat. "How did you die?"

"How do most hundred-and-four-year-old women

die?" Ms. McMartin asked. "Something gives out, and then something else gives out, and then something gives out that you really *need,* and then it's over." She gave a dainty shrug. "It was quite sudden, in the end. It didn't hurt."

"Oh," said Olive. "Good."

Ms. McMartin tilted her head sharply. A puzzled frown appeared on her features.

Olive cleared her throat again. "Um—there was a rumor that you were in here for a really long time before anybody found you. Someone even said . . . they said the cats had been *nibbling* on you."

"You know the cats, Olive," said Ms. McMartin, still frowning. "Does that sound like something they would do?"

"No," said Olive. "Well—maybe Harvey, if he—" She stopped herself. "No."

"As for it being 'a really long time' . . . It was a few days, I believe. Perhaps a week."

"So, you were all alone," Olive said. "When it happened."

Ms. McMartin stared into the fire and didn't answer.

Olive struggled on. "Didn't anybody—like Lucinda, or—didn't anyone miss you?"

Ms. McMartin's head jerked toward Olive. "Are you feeling *sorry for me,* Olive Dunwoody?" Her voice was clipped and cold. "No. No one missed me. Certainly not Lucinda Nivens."

Olive waited for a few seconds, breathing as quietly as she could.

Ms. McMartin's shade kept silent.

"Lucinda's brother—Morton—he's still here," Olive said at last. "In Elsewhere. He's trying to find his parents."

"Is that so?" Ms. McMartin sounded almost bored. "Good luck to him."

"You know where they are, don't you?" Olive gripped the arms of her chair so hard that the ancient wood squeaked in protest. "What did Aldous do to them?"

Ms. McMartin stared into the fire. Its light erased her eyes, leaving two shadowy pits behind. "Mary Nivens was dangerous to us," she said slowly. "Grandfather took her and her husband out of our way. He did what he had to do to keep this house and family safe."

Before her brain had the time to stop her mouth, Olive asked, "Is that what you told yourself when he killed your parents?"

Ms. McMartin's eyes flew back to Olive. Beyond the reach of the firelight, they were silvery and deep and cold. "There were very few things in this world that I loved," she said, in her soft, poisonous voice. "But I did love this house. In fact, this house may have been the *only* thing." Her mouth curved into a tiny smile. Annabelle's face, smooth and young, reappeared around it. "You understand that, don't you, Olive? You love it too." The smile widened. "And what about your parents? Do they love it as you do?"

"My—my parents are gone," said Olive. "They were taken from this house. And your portrait had something to do with it."

"Yes, she's loose, isn't she?" Ms. McMartin sounded amused. "I'm sure she's caused you all sorts of bother."

"Where do you think she would have taken them?" Olive asked, leaning forward, with her feet back on the floor. "And who do you think is helping her?"

"I don't know anything about it." Ms. McMartin waved one smoky hand. It moved beyond the beams of the firelight, and Olive saw it change into something black and withered—something that was barely a hand at all. Then Ms. McMartin folded her hands in her lap once again. "All I know for certain is that she wants this house back." Her eyes, shifting from an old woman's to Annabelle's, fixed on Olive. "Wouldn't you?"

"I—I don't—" Olive stammered.

"Tell the truth, Olive. Wouldn't you do almost anything—even dangerous, destructive things, things your friends warn you not to do, things that you don't truly understand—to keep this house for yourself?"

Olive's mouth fell open, but no words came out.

"Never mind," said Ms. McMartin, after a few silent seconds. "I think we both know the answer."

Olive jumped out of her chair so fast that its legs thumped against the floor. "Is that what you want to happen?" she demanded, stepping toward the flickering form in the other chair. "Do you want the younger version of *you* coming back to take over this house?" She leaned close enough to feel the chill surrounding Ms. McMartin, her words coming faster and faster. "I thought you changed your mind about all of that. I thought that was why you let your family die out in the end. I thought you might have *learned something* from all the horrible things you watched Aldous McMartin do!"

Ms. McMartin's eyes shifted away from Olive back to the fireplace. "I believe someone is at your door, Olive," she said softly. "You had better answer it."

Olive waited, rocking on her feet, but Ms. Martin didn't speak again until Olive had whirled around and stalked toward the door.

"Remember," she murmured, "I will be watching over *my house,* Olive Dunwoody."

Olive threw the library doors open with an aggravated double *bang.* She looked back over her shoulder, but the worn velvet chair before the fireplace was already empty. The fire smoldering in the grate had collapsed into a mass of ashes. Olive thought she could make out one more blotch of shadows gliding toward the darkened corner, but it moved quickly, and the room was too dim to be sure.

A silhouette that was too short to be Walter's or Delora's and too thin to be Mrs. Dewey's or Doctor Widdecombe's flickered outside of the front windows. Olive yanked the door open.

"I've been picking up some extremely odd thoughts from your vicinity," said Rutherford, without a hello. He hovered on the threshold, jiggling back and forth in his slippers. His jacket flapped loosely over his blue dragon pajamas. "I received flashes of candles and living shadows, and then for a while I was picking up a stream of mathematical equations, but that was interrupted by something about fire and Annabelle McMartin." His dark brown eyes honed on Olive's. "What, exactly, has been going on?"

"I must have been dreaming," said Olive lamely.

"Dreaming about Annabelle McMartin and the quadratic formula?"

"They were really bad dreams," said Olive.

"And where is Walter?" asked Rutherford, looking unconvinced. "Why isn't he standing guard?"

"Umm . . ." Olive hesitated. She glanced around the hallway, where patches of living darkness huddled in each corner and cranny. "Come with me." She grabbed Rutherford by the sleeve of his jacket and hustled him down the hall, across the kitchen, and out the door of the back porch. She halted inside the pool of the burning porch light that spilled over the threshold, where she hoped no shades could follow.

Above the backyard, a fragment of moon was wedged deep in a grape jelly sky. Wind whispered over the grass, scattering clusters of dead leaves. To their right, beyond the lilac hedge, the Nivens house towered, dark and silent.

"Rutherford," Olive whispered, "you can't tell your grandmother about this, all right?"

Rutherford raised his right hand. "I swear upon my honor that I shall—"

"Good," Olive interrupted. "That magic that Delora mentioned? The kind your grandmother said we shouldn't try? Well . . . I asked her and Doctor Widdecombe to help me do it."

Even through their dirty lenses, Olive could see Rutherford's eyes widen. "The necromantic conjuration and expulsion?"

"The . . . what?"

"It means getting rid of the power of the dead, to put it simply. Doctor Widdecombe prefers the term 'necromantic conjuration and expulsion.' Was it successful?"

"Well . . . sort of." Olive rubbed the sleeves of her sweater, trying to brush away the chill of the deepening night. "The conjuration part worked, I guess. But the other part—"

"The expulsion?"

"—didn't."

"Oh," said Rutherford slowly. His eyes traveled toward the well-lit windows above them, and then back to Olive's face. "What did Doctor Widdecombe try to do to aid the expulsion process?"

Olive blinked. "Nothing."

"Nothing?" Rutherford echoed.

"All right, not *nothing*. He screamed so loudly that he might have popped his own eardrums, and then he ran out of the house before Delora could catch up with him."

One of Rutherford's eyebrows went up. "I find that rather difficult to believe," he said, like a parent answering a toddler who insists that there's an eight-headed monster hiding under the bed. "Doctor Widdecombe is a world-renowned expert on magic in nearly all its forms."

"He's also a scaredy-cat," said Olive. "And so is Delora."

Rutherford tilted his head doubtfully.

"Just because he's some famous expert—"

"A *world-renowned* expert," Rutherford corrected.

"That doesn't mean he knows *everything*," said Olive, folding her arms across her chest. "I mean, when you read his thoughts, you must notice that they're not always perfect."

Rutherford tilted his head to the other side. "Olive, I have never read anything in his thoughts that didn't confirm what I already know: Namely, that he is an expert on magical history who has nothing but the best intentions when it comes to . . ." Rutherford's words slowed. His eyes grew distant. ". . . The Fibonacci sequence."

"The *what* sequence?" asked Olive.

"What?" said Rutherford.

"Why did you start talking about a sequence?"

Rutherford blinked. "I didn't. *You* did."

"I only said what *you* said," Olive argued. "I don't even know what the fettuccini sequence is!"

"The *Fibonacci* sequence," Rutherford corrected. "It's named after a medieval mathematician, and it's a series of numbers in which the next number is always the sum of the two preceding numbers. It frequently appears in nature: in ferns, in seashells, in pinecones—"

"All right," Olive interrupted. "But I didn't say it." She paused, staring through the dimness into Rutherford's brown eyes. "If it's a math term, do you think it could have been coming from someone else? Like . . . maybe . . . from my parents?"

Rutherford gave her a thoughtful frown. "I don't see how that would be possible. I can only read thoughts from a distance when I know the thinker extremely well—like you, or my grandmother, or my own parents. I generally need to look directly into someone's face in order to read them."

"But Delora said they were nearby, didn't she?" Olive's eyes raked the yard. Leaves covered the garden with thick, grave-like mounds. Shadows pooled around the porch steps. "What if we just missed them somehow? Or what if they've been hidden in more than one place, and now they've been moved to a spot that we haven't checked again?" Olive's heart jumped a little higher with each question. "You search the yard, and I'll look through the nearest rooms! Let's go!"

As Rutherford hurried away, Olive lunged into the kitchen, yanking open each cupboard and drawer. She checked the downstairs bathroom, avoiding the grasping shade that rippled behind the door, and looked under all the furniture in the dining room and parlor.

Rutherford was waiting for her on the back porch when she returned.

"I searched the shed, the lawn, and the crawl space underneath the porch," he announced, peeling an old spiderweb from one sleeve. "I found nothing."

"Me too." Olive gave an exasperated sigh. "Do you think we're getting close? Are you reading anything else?"

Rutherford shook his head. "Nothing but you running through a checklist of searched spots."

"I don't get it." Olive flopped against the doorframe, the hope that had lightened her leaking away. She gazed out over the withered lawn, and felt the cold, and the darkness, and the *hugeness* of the night looming all around her. "If they're so close, then where could they be?"

Rutherford adjusted his smudgy glasses. "There is one positive factor to keep in mind," he said, shuffling nearer to Olive. "If it is your parents that I'm reading, it means that they're still alive."

"I suppose," said Olive, not feeling very comforted.

Rutherford tensed. "My grandmother just woke up," he whispered. "She fell asleep on the couch with a book, and I was supposed to be in bed an hour ago."

"Remember," said Olive as Rutherford darted toward the hedge, "don't tell her about the—the congregation and exception—"

"The conjuration and expulsion."

"*That.* Not yet. She would probably blame Delora and Doctor Widdecombe for trying it, but it was really my fault, because . . ." Olive's mind traveled back to the painting of Linden Street, where memories of the Calling Candle and Leopold and Annabelle were waiting. ". . . Because I did some stupid things today."

"I am aware of that," said Rutherford. "I should be able to make up an excuse to keep her away for a while.

Besides, she and Doctor Widdecombe and Delora are casting some Seeking Spells tomorrow, so they will all be occupied." Rutherford gave Olive a last sharp look. "If you need me, let me know," he added. With a courtly bow, he shoved his way through the barren lilac hedge and hustled away into the dark.

Locking the heavy back door behind her, Olive shuffled down the hall. She glanced into the library, the only downstairs room that she'd left unlit. A black shape—a shape like a horse, but with an alligator's long, pointed teeth filling its jaws—galloped out of the shadows straight toward her. Olive flicked on the library's chandelier. The horse vanished, leaving the smoky outline of a gaunt man with thick sideburns. He glowered at Olive, backing toward the wall until he seeped into its stones.

The clock in the entryway played its soft song. Eleven o'clock: well past Olive's bedtime. Olive paused on the staircase, listening to the last chime ring away through the lifeless rooms. And then even the echoes died away.

Having Walter lurking around the house had been uncomfortable, but at least she hadn't been alone overnight. Olive's chest started to ache. Now the house was one huge, empty reminder of everything that wasn't there. She missed the sound of her father's toothbrush tapping the sink—always an even number of times. She missed her mother peeping through her bedroom door to wish her good night. She missed the soft sound of her parents talking, lulling her to sleep from the other end of the hall.

But her parents were gone. The neighbors had fled. Leopold was in the hands of her enemy.

"Horatio?" Olive called, hating the way her voice sounded in this huge, hollow house, too loud and too small at the same time. "Harvey?"

There was no answer.

Maybe the other cats had left her as well. Maybe they had never come back inside the house after Walter had drawn them out of it. Or maybe they were hiding somewhere, frightened and furious. Maybe they were hiding from *her*.

Olive hurried along the upstairs hall, switching on more lights as she went. Shades hissed and whispered in the corners. In her own bedroom, even with all the lights on, the space under her bed was dark. A pair of shadowy hands reached out from beneath the dust ruffle. Olive spotted the tip of a scaly tail under her closet door. Even if she knew that the shades couldn't hurt her, there was no way that she could sleep here tonight.

How could she ever sleep again?

Olive stared at Hershel, the worn brown bear lying limply on her pillows, and felt her throat clench.

It was time to give up. Everything she had done to solve her problems—releasing the shades, using the Calling Candle, even taking Morton out for Halloween—had only made the problems worse. Her arms were filled with cement. Her legs were like lead. She was tired, and hopeless, and it was time to set the weight of this big stone house down.

Olive took a heavy breath. She could still go Elsewhere. She could climb into the painting of Linden Street, and curl up on Morton's quiet front porch, and go to sleep. By the time she woke up, it would all be over. She wouldn't have won the fight . . . but at least the fight would be done.

With a little good-bye wave to Hershel, Olive stepped back into the hall. She arranged the spectacles carefully on her nose. *I keep trusting the wrong people,* she thought, dragging her body over the bottom of the thick gold frame. Trusting herself had been one more mistake. She had scared away the neighbors, lost Leopold, and failed her parents. It was time for her to get out of the way, before anyone else got hurt.

"Olive!" shouted a distant voice.

But Olive had already fallen through the frame.

18

"OLIVE!" THE VOICE shouted again. "Olive!"

It wasn't until the third shout that Olive realized the voice came from *inside* the frame. And the voice was growing louder, or closer, or both. She blinked up from the misty grass into a pair of bright green eyes.

"Olive," gasped Horatio. "Are you all right?"

"Horatio!" Olive sat up. "I'm so glad to see you!" She threw both arms around the huge orange cat and gave him a passionate squeeze. "You weren't trying to hide from me?"

"From *you?* What a ridiculous idea," said the cat, squirming unappreciatively in Olive's arms. "Why would we want to get away from you?" With a final squirm, he leaped back to the ground. "We picked this painting precisely because you were likely to visit it."

"So Harvey is here too? Oh, good." Olive let out a sigh of relief. "I was sure you were angry at me."

Horatio stopped smoothing his hug-rumpled fur and gave Olive a sharp look. "A logical conclusion," he snapped. "Tricking your allies in order to proceed with a *truly IDIOTIC plan* might indeed leave those allies the slightest bit irritated." Horatio released a slow breath. "But I am *not* angry at you, Olive," he went on, more calmly. "And I'll tell you why: Next to the mess you're in, my anger will seem about as threatening as a stick in a swordfight. And you will have to deal with that mess *on your own*."

"On my own?" Olive repeated in a small voice. "But—why?"

Horatio stared up at Olive from the mist, his eyes glittering. "The shades are a part of this house," he said. "And we *belong* to this house."

"You mean, they could still control you?"

"They would certainly try." Horatio gave his whiskers a tense stroke. "That's why we must remain Elsewhere for the time being. This house—and the McMartin family—is searching for an heir. It needs someone to use its power. It will manipulate, or influence, or corrupt anyone it can."

Olive bit the inside of her cheek. Another wave of hopelessness made her eyes sting. "But if this house will try to turn everyone against me . . . then who can I trust?" she whispered.

Horatio watched her. His green eyes softened slightly. "Perhaps you should trust Olive Dunwoody," he said, after several quiet seconds. "That's what *I* am going to do."

Morton and Harvey were waiting for them on the porch of the tall gray house. Morton sat on the steps, kicking a pebble that zoomed back to his toes again and again. Harvey leaned against the railing nearby. He was wearing his coffee can helmet, but it had been turned around so that the eyehole revealed a splotchy patch of the back of his head.

"Is that you, Olive?" Harvey asked in a muffled voice. "How kind you are, to visit me in the cell where I have been unfairly imprisoned by this conspiracy!"

"Why does he have his helmet on backward?" Olive whispered to Horatio.

"Have you ever seen *The Man in the Iron Mask*?" Horatio whispered back.

"No."

"Don't bother."

"How long must this go on?" Harvey wailed from inside the can, banging his head tinnily against the wooden rails. "How long will evil reign? How long must I, the rightful leader of my homeland, wait for justice?"

"'Rightful leader'?" Horatio repeated. "I think the world would be a rather different place if France were led by a cat with his head in a coffee can."

"Morton," said Olive, "I have a lot to tell you, about—"

"About the Calling Candle and Leopold and the shades. I already know," said Morton, folding his arms importantly.

"Oh," said Olive. "Good."

"So, what are you going to do?" Morton asked.

"I don't know."

Morton looked back down at his toes. He gave the pebble another I-don't-really-care-about-any-of-this kick. "Are you going to leave?"

Horatio stared up at her. Subtly, Harvey turned his coffee can until one eye peered through its eyehole.

"No," said Olive. "This is our house. I'm not giving up." She sank down next to Morton on the steps. "I just wish there weren't so many problems at once. One problem is stacked on top of another problem, and there's another problem under that, and I don't even know where to start."

"Start at the beginning," said Morton.

Olive gave him a little smile. "That's what my dad would say. 'Start at the beginning. Retrace your steps.'"

Leaning her chin on her knee, Olive pushed her mind back through the awful week. She moved past the hideous shades, and Ms. McMartin's hollow eyes, and Annabelle's smile as she walked off with Leopold in her arms, and Walter lurking around the corners, to the spot where it had all began: in a heap of spilled candy at the foot of the stairs. "My parents," she murmured. "That's where it began."

"Good," said Horatio. "And what's the next question?"

"We know *who* took them," said Olive. "But we don't know *why*. If the McMartins are trying to get us out of their house, why wouldn't they take me too? Unless . . ." Olive paused as a door creaked open in the back of her mind. "Unless they had some other reason to want my parents. If there was something my parents could do that I couldn't . . ."

Olive jumped to her feet. "I know where to start!"

she shouted, already tearing toward the deserted street. "Thank you!"

"Good luck, Olive!" shouted Morton behind her.

"Be careful!" called Horatio.

Harvey's words—"Go, with the blessings of the rightful king of France!"—followed her over the misty grass and through the picture frame.

Olive thundered down the stairs. It was nearly midnight now, and the sky beyond the windows was black and starless. Sticking to well-lighted spots, Olive skidded across the entryway and through the library's wooden doors.

The brass chandelier glowed reassuringly above her. Still, the edges of the room flickered with shadows of beastly bodies and groping limbs. Cold air trailed along the walls. Dozens of eyes followed Olive to her mother's desk.

Stacks of papers waited on the desktop, already gathering a thin coat of dust. Being careful to keep the pages in order, Olive flipped through the first stack. The papers were covered with her mother's neat handwriting, some of it forming actual words, some of it dissolving into chains of symbols that could have meant anything at all. Could this have something to do with magic?

Olive moved to her father's desk. She set aside a pile of students' quizzes and picked up the notebook underneath. It was filled with symbols and scribbles, this time in her father's loopy handwriting. Olive squinted down at one mark that looked like a picnic table lying on its side, and another that looked like a cherry bomb with a bent wick. Could she be staring at the explanation without even seeing it?

Olive was still frowning down at the chain of squiggles when the entire page went black.

A breath caught in Olive's throat.

The chandelier had gone out. So had the lights in the hall, and in the front parlor, whose entrance she could see through the library's open doors. Even without looking, Olive knew the other rooms would be the same. The entire house had gone dark.

Around her, the air came alive. Gusts of cold burst from the walls. Sinuous, scaly forms swam around her in the blackness. Something with horns sprouting from its massive head loomed over her left shoulder, while something with an insect's rippling legs scuttled up her right arm. Dropping the notebook onto the desk, Olive backed away, shaking her arm until the crawling thing dropped off.

"Get out," she heard the inhuman voices hiss and mutter around her.

If she could make it to the wall, she could test the light switch. If the power had gone out—or been cut off—she would have to run to the kitchen, through the crowded, crawling blackness, to find a flashlight. Olive kept her head down, blocking out the voices, and made a beeline for the wall. She had only a few more steps to go when a tall, dark figure—too solid and too human to be a shade—loomed through the open double doors.

Olive froze.

The figure in the doorway didn't seem to see her. It wavered for a moment, its hooded head swiveling from side to side, surveying the huge, dark room. Then it glided into the library, its long cloak rustling over the floor.

The air around Olive grew instantly warmer. She felt claws and tails and slippery limbs sliding past her as the shades moved away, following the intruder. Olive watched a clot of shadow drift across the room toward the bookshelves, its blackness so thick that it seemed to pull in every last mote of light; to swallow it, like a huge, hungry mouth. Olive saw it envelop the hooded figure. Holding her breath, she inched backward, toward the doors.

Across the room, voices muttered, growing louder and louder. Olive caught fragments of their words. *This house . . . Join . . . Power . . .*

Olive felt her shoulder bump against the wall. The tiny scuff of sweater meeting wood made her heart stand still, but the hooded figure—Annabelle, or Aldous, or someone else—didn't seem to hear it.

Olive was just about to duck out the door and make a run for it when from across the room, there came a soft *click*. A round blotch of light traveled across the bookshelves, glimmering on the embossed spines. The shades backed out of reach of the beam, growling and hissing angrily. Aldous and Annabelle wouldn't have needed a light to find something inside of their own house, would they? And would either of them have carried a *flashlight?*

Olive swept one arm along the wall. Her fingers brushed the light switch.

It won't work, she told herself. *Of course it won't. It won't—*

The chandelier flared.

A burst of warm gold light filled the library. The McMartin shades thinned to wispy human outlines, scattering into the shadows.

The hooded figure dropped its flashlight. It hit the rug with a thump.

Olive took a tentative step forward. The figure kept its back to her, its now-empty hands in the air, as though an imaginary police officer had just shouted *Halt!*

Frowning now, Olive strode across the room. With each step she recognized another detail: the tattered gray robes, the long, bony hands, the narrow, hunching shoulders.

She grabbed the intruder by the sleeve.

Walter spun around, blinking down at Olive from the depths of the ghoul's hood.

"Walter!" The name burst out of Olive like a small explosion. "What are you doing back here? I thought you were one of the McMartins!"

Walter blinked down at her. His Adam's apple bobbed wildly.

"What were you looking for?" Olive glanced up at the bookshelves. "And why would you sneak back in here, instead of just . . ." The air gushed out of her lungs. "Wait a minute," she whispered. "You were going to steal something. Something you knew no one would want you to have. Weren't you?"

"Mmm . . ." said Walter. His eyes blinked even faster.

A sudden frost filled Olive's body. She was too numb to be angry or frightened now; she was merely cold. Cold and hard. "Was it the grimoire?" she asked. "Or something else that belonged to the McMartins? Is that why you were snooping around all week, looking through the books, searching the garden?"

"Mmm . . ." Walter mumbled again. He took a step backward, colliding with the bookshelf. "Mmm . . . yes, but . . ."

"Why?" Olive asked, staring up into Walter's face. He couldn't meet her eyes. "Never mind," she said slowly. "I know why. You wanted this house. You wanted its secrets for yourself, to show your aunt and uncle what a great magician you could be." She glanced at the pool of shadows lurking in the corner. The frost grew thicker, hardening her skin, turning her spine into steel. "You were working with *them,*" she said. "You were going to help them get this house back, if they would make you their heir."

"No," said Walter, speaking clearly for the first time. "I swear. I—mmm—I just needed something."

"What?"

Walter's Adam's apple bounced like a bobber on a fishing line. "I—I can't tell you."

"If you can't even tell me what it is, how am I supposed to believe you?" Olive frowned up at Walter. She folded her arms across her chest, squeezing herself as tight as she could. This didn't help her feel any less alone.

Walter didn't answer.

"I don't know what to do," Olive said at last. "Should I put you into Elsewhere and leave you there? Should I call your aunt and uncle and Mrs. Dewey, and tell them all about—"

"No!" Walter interrupted. Fear glittered in his eyes. "Please. No. Don't—don't do that."

Olive shook her head, letting out another angry breath. "I *knew* I couldn't trust you," she whispered.

Walter's shoulders sank. His mouth twitched. For a moment, he looked as though he was about to say something, but then he closed his eyes and swallowed, and whatever words had been waiting slipped back down his throat.

"Here's what I'm going to do to you," said Olive, after a long, quiet moment. Walter stared at her, clearly terrified. "I'm going to let you leave." Walter's eyes grew even wider. "But you can *never* enter this house again. If I even think you've tried, I'll tell your aunt about all of this."

"Thank you," Walter gushed. He ducked past Olive, the ghoul's robes fluttering around him. "Thank you." In a few quick strides, he was out of the library and through the front door. It hung open behind him, letting in the night air.

Feeling suddenly defrosted and empty, Olive trailed across the room. The hallway beyond still lay in darkness. She hadn't had time to reach for the next light switch when a shadow entered the beam of light that fell through the library doors.

Olive glanced up at the gray woman's string of pearls and deep, cold eyes. She took a startled step back.

"An interesting choice, Olive Dunwoody," said the shade of Ms. McMartin. "Letting your enemy go free. I thought you would wish to protect this house."

"I—I *do*," Olive stammered. "But I won't be like you. I won't—"

Before she could finish, the misty figure had drifted back into the blackness, its face dissolving, its pearls fading like something sinking into a deep lake.

Shuddering, Olive dashed from the glow of the library to the front door, flicking on the entry lights. In their sconces, dusty bulbs flickered to life along the hall. For a second, Olive wondered how Walter had managed to shut off all of the lights at once—but maybe he knew something about fuses and breakers that Olive didn't. (If he knew what fuses and breakers actually *were,* he would have been ahead of Olive.) She stood on the threshold for a moment, listening to the rusty creak of the porch swing and watching the synthetic cobwebs sway between the pillars. Behind her, the house was quiet and lifeless once again.

With a sigh, she reached for the doorknob. Her fingers had just closed around the chilly metal when a voice from the darkness murmured, "You shouldn't have done that, Olive."

Rutherford stepped out of the porch's shadows. A streak of moonlight glinted on his glasses, turning them into two smaller, fingerprint-smudged moons.

"You shouldn't have let Walter go," he said. "He knows where your parents are."

"I SAW IT," RUTHERFORD whispered. "In his thoughts."

They were huddled against the porch's inner corner, next to the softly groaning swing, and Rutherford was speaking so fast that at first Olive thought he'd said "I saw wet tennis thoughts," which didn't make any sense at all.

"I was certain that Walter was worthy of our trust, but I was misled, and I give you my deepest apologies," Rutherford rushed on. "But I'm sure I'm not being misled now. He knows where your parents are—although I couldn't read anything about the precise location. I'd just come over here to check on you, because I could read very clearly that something had gone wrong, and when Walter ran past me on his way out the door, I caught a fragment of his thoughts. He *knows* something!" Rutherford finished, jiggling back and forth so fast that his face was only a moonlit blur.

For the first time in days, Olive felt a spark of pure hope. Walter *knew* something! Something that might bring her parents home at last!

"We need to find out what he knows," Olive whispered back.

"In order to pick up additional information, I would need to get closer to him," said Rutherford. "Which would mean sneaking into the house next door."

"Let's go!" Olive shot toward the porch steps, and halted with one foot over the edge. "Wait. If we leave, there will be no one guarding the house. The cats are Elsewhere. They won't come out as long as the McMartins' shades are loose."

"Perhaps I could go alone . . ." said Rutherford, his jiggling starting to slow.

"No. We'll be safer together." Olive chewed on her lower lip. "We'll just have to get in and out as fast as we can."

"An excellent plan," Rutherford whispered back.

With Olive leading the way, they slipped around the side of the old stone house and through the lilac hedge. Shriveled twigs clacked and rattled around them. The tall gray house waited on the other side, as cold and quiet as a gravestone. As they inched closer, Olive spotted a fragile red glow behind one curtained window, and knew that the old glass lamps were burning in the study.

"Here is an eventuality I did not consider," Rutherford whispered as he and Olive pressed their backs to the cold gray wall. "How do we get in? The doors are protected by a voice-released locking spell. We saw Walter use it on Halloween, remember?"

Olive's eyes traveled along the wall to the edge of the front porch. "What if we climbed from the railings up onto the porch roof, and then went in through the broken window in Lucinda's old bedroom?"

"Are you sure that's safe?" Rutherford asked. The faint moonlight revealed his worried face.

"No," said Olive. "But I'm going to try it anyway."

As quietly as she could manage, Olive hauled herself onto the porch railing, teetering along its narrow wooden beam. She wrapped her chilly fingers around the roof's edge. From there, she managed to swing one leg up over the roof, and then to roll the rest of her body up to safety, being careful not to crush the spectacles. She reached back down for Rutherford's hand.

They crawled across the leaf-strewn roof. The curtains in the shattered window drifted softly over the sill before them, snagging now and then on the remaining bits of glass that jutted around the frame like carnivorous teeth. Cautiously, Olive and Rutherford climbed over the shards and through the empty window.

Inside what had been Lucinda's bedroom, the air felt even colder than it had outside. Dead leaves cluttered the corners. Rain had faded the delicate curtains, and discolored patches had formed on the once-polished floor. The scorched spot where Annabelle had turned Lucinda into a burst of oily flames remained on the boards, dark and deep enough to be seen even in the weak moonlight.

"We'll have to be careful as we go downstairs," Rutherford whispered, pausing in the bedroom's open doorway. "There might be other protective spells in place."

"All right," Olive whispered back. "And from this point on, no talking, unless it's absolutely necessary."

"A vow of silence. I agree." Rutherford held up one hand, oath-taking-style, before treading softly into the hall.

Without any windows, and with no lights filtering up from the floor below, the hallway was as dim as the inside of an oilcan. Olive pressed her spine to the wall, feeling the deep chill of the house penetrate through her sweater. For the first time in decades, living people were occupying this house—and yet, with its neglected, chilly rooms and pitch-black corridors, the house felt more lifeless than ever.

Olive started down the wooden staircase, inching her toes over each step, and setting her feet down as lightly as she could. In the darkness, it was impossible to tell where one step ended and the next began, but at last her toes hit a patch of floor that didn't have an edge.

Keeping silent, Olive and Rutherford glided along the downstairs hallway. Here, all of the curtains had been closed, so no lights from the street or sky could lessen the corridor's darkness. They had to navigate by touch until they rounded a corner, and a slip of warm red light spilled across a patch of the hardwood floor.

They had reached the dining room.

A soft crackle of fire came from within, along with the sound of familiar voices. Olive and Rutherford leaned in, pressing their ears to the door's chilly surface.

". . . ever did you hope to accomplish by creeping into that house in the middle of the night?" Doctor Widdecombe's voice was saying, quite loudly.

"Mmm . . . just some ingredients . . ." said Walter's much deeper, much quieter voice. "Shifting Seed. Things for transformational spells."

"Transformational spells?" boomed Doctor Widdecombe. "It's fortunate that you didn't find any Shifting Seed! You might have turned yourself into a ninety-eight-pound toad!"

"And that poor child," breathed Delora's voice. "If you'd woken her, can you imagine how frightened she would have been? She has quite enough fear to deal with in that house today."

"It was terrifying enough when you woke *us,* bursting back in here like the world's worst cat burglar," put in Doctor Widdecombe.

"Sorry . . . mmm . . ." Walter's voice muttered something too low for Olive to catch.

"Yes, well, when we have determined how to rid the house of the shades—a pursuit in which your aunt and I are both fully engaged—we will have to reconsider whether you are fit to act as Olive's guard after all."

Olive hung on each word, biting her lips to keep silent. Her heart was thundering, and her breath was coming faster, and a little piece of hair had slipped inside her ear and was itching and tickling irritatingly. What a liar Walter was! She could open this door right now and proclaim to Doctor Widdecombe and Delora that Walter was a traitor, ready to turn against them all. She gritted her teeth. The itch in her ear mixed with her simmering anger, and suddenly, Olive was boiling over. She had just grabbed the doorknob, when Rutherford's fingers locked around her wrist.

"What?" Olive mouthed.

Rutherford shook his head emphatically. He tugged her away from the door, along the hall, toward the kitchen. Olive trailed him through the blackness, chewing the inside of her cheek in a fury.

At the far corner of the kitchen, where the voices from the dining room could no longer reach them, Rutherford stopped.

"What *is* it?" Olive demanded through clenched teeth.

"What were you thinking, Olive?" Rutherford whispered. "Why were you about to give us away before we've ascertained what has been going on?"

"Because," said Olive, in a much louder whisper, "we should just tell Delora and Doctor Widdecombe that Walter is lying. *They* can deal with him!"

"Is that what you meant about 'knowing the answers'?"

"The answers to what?" Olive whispered back.

"Didn't you think something about *knowing the answers?*"

"No. I was thinking, *We should go in there and tell everybody the truth,* and that's what I'm still thinking right now!"

Olive turned back toward the hall, but Rutherford caught her by the arm.

"I'm absolutely certain that I heard those words. Although, come to think of it, it *didn't* sound like your usual thoughts. But it came from somewhere close by."

Olive frowned. "Did you hear anything else?"

"Something about Aristotle . . . displacement . . . a blue bath towel . . ."

Olive's heart shot upward, fizzing against her ribs like an exploding pop bottle. She grabbed Rutherford's arm with both hands.

"I don't know what that means, so don't ask me," he said defensively.

"I do!" Olive cried. *"It's my dad!"* She choked back her excitement, forcing it into a whisper. "Can you tell where it came from?"

"No, nothing about its surroundings. But if we get closer to the source, I may be able to read more clearly."

"Then go!" whispered Olive, using every bit of her willpower to keep herself from shouting instead.

Rutherford swayed, listening, his shoes creaking softly on the kitchen floor. Then he took off for the hall, with Olive hanging on to his sleeve.

They hurried past the dining room door, where arguing voices could still be heard, and along the edge of Lucinda's perfect white parlor and around the foot of the staircase. One tiny window set in the front door wasn't covered by a curtain, and the pale glow of moon, stars, and streetlamps tinged the nearest few feet of the hall.

"I don't think the source is upstairs," said Rutherford slowly. "And, Olive, thinking *hurry up* over and over again is not actually helpful."

"Then just *hurry up*," said Olive.

As Olive tiptoed behind, Rutherford crept to the other side of the hall, around the barricade formed by the staircase, where three closed doors made darker rectangles in the wall. He passed the first door, hesitated, then darted toward the second. It groaned softly on its hinges as he pulled it open.

Inside, the room was utterly dark. There were no windows, not even covered by curtains, and no other sources of light. Nothing glinted or glimmered in the distant glow from the front door.

"Well," whispered Rutherford bravely, "I shall go first." He edged through the open door.

With a deep breath, Olive followed. She shut the door quietly behind them.

Within the blackness, Olive stretched her arms out, testing the air. She hadn't taken two steps before she hit something with her fingers—something soft and furry, and then something heavy and rough, and then something that felt like silk. Beside her, she could hear Rutherford rustling through the fabric too.

"We must be in a closet," Olive whispered, patting at the wall of cloth. Her hands traveled up, still patting and poking, until suddenly they were patting and poking at something not made of fabric at all.

The thing was about the size of a basketball, but lumpier and slicker. The ridge of one large bump stuck out of one side. Beside the bump were two matching pits, which led down to cheeks, which thrust outward into something that was not a nose, but a *muzzle*: a long, tooth-filled maw.

Olive let out a shriek, muffling it in her sleeve a second too late.

"What is it?" Rutherford's worried voice asked, from somewhere in the darkness.

"It's a severed head!" Olive squeaked. Diving toward the door, she groped along the walls, searching for a light switch. She found one just to the right of the doorway, but when she tried to turn it on: Nothing. She flipped the switch again and again, as a growing panic buzzed through her body. *Of course,* Olive realized. The lights *wouldn't* work in a house where no one had paid the electric bill for months, but she was still stubbornly jiggling the switch when a needle of blue-white light poked through the darkness.

"Did you say 'a severed head'?" Rutherford whispered, aiming the miniature flashlight at Olive's face.

"Why didn't you say you had a flashlight?" Olive hissed back.

"Because I knew we could only use it in dire circumstances, or the light would make us too easily detectable," Rutherford explained, swinging the beam across the room.

They were indeed in a closet: a well-stuffed storage closet the size of a small bedroom. A row of clothes—

old wool coats and velvet cloaks and silky robes—made a solid wall of fabric ahead of them. And on the shelf just above the clothes was a bumpy, hollow-eyed, rubbery face.

Olive stepped closer. The face was made of plastic, with holes for eyes, and rows of molded, snarling teeth. "It's just a mask," she breathed. "A werewolf mask."

A werewolf mask.

Olive's memory shot to the painting in the kitchen, where the stonemasons worked on their never-finished wall. They had seen monsters—three or four monsters—hurry through the old stone house on Halloween night. They had mentioned werewolves, Olive was sure of it. She remembered the second builder's nervous voice. *And there was a mummy. . .*

Olive lunged toward the closet's high shelf, groping along it until she found another mask: a second werewolf. Behind it was the deflated face of another werewolf. And then, finally, a mummy mask, with everything but its empty eyeholes covered in strips of rubber bandages.

"Four masks," said Olive. "Two for my parents. That would leave one for Walter, and one for Annabelle." Olive looked up at Rutherford, who was peering over her shoulder. "Did Walter have the chance to change costumes that night? Or was there *another* person helping Annabelle? Three werewolves, plus one mummy, plus one ghoul . . ."

"Wait," Rutherford whispered. "Say that again."

"Three werewolves, plus one mummy, plus one ghoul—"

"Three plus one plus one is five," Rutherford interrupted, his eyes going distant. "Three and five are both prime numbers. One is not generally considered a prime number."

A breath caught in Olive's lungs. She felt her rib cage expand, as if there wasn't room inside for all of that air and her beating, bouncing heart.

"The list of primes, excluding one, is as follows: two, three, five, seven, eleven, thirteen, seventeen, nineteen . . ." Rutherford's voice sped quickly on, while his body swiveled slowly back to the row of clothes. ". . . twenty-three, twenty-nine, thirty-one, thirty-seven . . ."

With both arms, Olive thrust the clothes apart.

The closet extended far beyond the rack of clothes. A deep, narrow space dwindled away before them, its dark walls lined with stacks of old hatboxes and leather trunks. In the distance, nearly hidden behind a wall of boxes, were two big brocade armchairs.

Two armchairs that were occupied by Mr. and Mrs. Dunwoody.

By the narrow beam of Rutherford's flashlight, Olive could see that her parents' eyes were closed, and their heads were flopped back against the chair cushions. Mr. Dunwoody's face looked oddly naked without his thick glasses, but otherwise, her parents looked perfectly normal. And perfectly *alive*.

"Dad!" Olive cried. "Mom!"

She dove into the back of the closet, knocking down the boxes, sending stacks of storage spilling across the floor.

"Perhaps you should keep your voice down, Olive," Rutherford whispered.

But Olive wasn't listening.

"Mom!" She shook her mother's arm, feeling its warm, wonderful alive-ness even through its cardigan sleeve. The arm flopped back over the armrest the moment Olive released it. She grabbed Mr. Dunwoody's hand. "Dad, can you hear me?"

"They appear to be under some sort of sleeping spell," said Rutherford as Mr. Dunwoody let out a resonant snore. "Perhaps that explains why I was able to read their thoughts, even from a greater distance."

"It certainly explains why Walter was rooting around in our garden!" Olive growled, her happiness sliding back into anger. "Let's get Doctor Widdecombe and Delora, and they can help—"

There was a creak of disused hinges. A flicker of firelight filled the opening closet door.

Doctor Widdecombe stood in the doorway. Delora, holding a glass-shaded lamp, hovered in the hall behind him. Their faces wore matching expressions of worry and surprise.

"Delora!" Olive stumbled over the heaps of boxes, rushing toward the door. "Doctor Widdecombe! *Walter* is the one who took my parents!"

Doctor Widdecombe looked down at Olive. His worried eyes began to crinkle, and his beard began to twitch, and then he placed both hands on his belly and let out a long, jolly chuckle. Delora smiled in spite of herself, hiding her mouth behind one pale hand.

"Walter?" repeated Doctor Widdecombe, between hearty *Ho-ho-ha's.* "You think *Walter* could manage such a thing, in secrecy, with *or* without the help of a greater magician?" He laughed once more—*Ha-ho-hoom*—and then patted his belly in a contented way. "No, Olive," he said, still smiling cheerily down at her. "*We* are the ones who took your parents."

NEXT TO OLIVE, Rutherford froze. The beam of his flashlight had come to rest on Doctor Widdecombe's tweed lapel, and it stayed there, casting its bluish light over the edge of the professor's round, smiling face.

Olive's arrangement of thoughts, everything she knew or thought she knew, slipped out of place and tumbled downward, filling her brain with a shattered mess. "What?" she said. "But—*why?*"

"Our plan was, as *you* were the only inhabitant who knew everything about the McMartin house," Doctor Widdecombe began, "to remove your parents, and then to let you lead us directly to the house's most valuable secrets—the familiars, the grimoire, Elsewhere and how to enter it, the ingredients for Aldous's paints, and so forth. You proved to be extremely stubborn about sharing these things, however. So our next course of action involved removing *you*." He folded his hands behind his back, still smiling. "If you vacated the house, we would have time to search it in perfect privacy, at our leisure. With your parents gone, we assumed that you too would wish to leave the house—to stay with Mrs. Dewey, perhaps. In time, we would have reunited you with your family, someplace safely far from here."

"But you just wouldn't *leave*," Delora put in, widening her silvery eyes.

"Yes, you turned out to be astonishingly stubborn," said Doctor Widdecombe pleasantly. "Our plan was to draw the McMartin shades out of their resting places and set them loose in the house, which we successfully did. And *still*, even with your house full of those hateful things, you refused to depart." Doctor Widdecombe gave an aggravated little shake of his head. "We were discussing our next move—something that wouldn't require the destruction or weakening of the house itself, of course—when we were interrupted by tonight's intrusions. And here we are." Doctor Widdecombe smiled down at the two of them, joggling gently on his feet.

Rutherford had been staring, slack-jawed, at the professor. His mouth slammed shut with an audible click. "It was *you*?" he asked. "An expert on magical history, and an academically honored author?" His voice grew louder and faster. "You deceived us!" he shouted. "Olive, my grandmother; all of us!" He stepped closer to Doctor Widdecombe, his eyes coming in line with the professor's straining coat buttons. "Why couldn't I tell that you were plotting against us?" he demanded. "I've read your thoughts for days now, and—"

"And learned nothing; yes, I know," said Doctor Widdecombe mildly. "You see, we were well aware that you were a reader long before we arrived on Linden Street. It is not so difficult for accomplished witches like ourselves to control our thoughts while in your vicinity, to avoid eye contact, and so forth. I did dislike deceiving you," he went on, sounding almost apologetic. "You are a talented boy. Don't let this failure discourage you."

Rutherford looked as though he might explode.

"But *why?*" Olive asked, moving to Rutherford's side. "Why did you do this?" She glanced back at her parents' faces, still fast asleep in the flickering lamplight. "Are you working for Annabelle?"

"Goodness, no," said Delora.

"We would like to be rid of her as much as you would, Olive." Doctor Widdecombe brought his face closer to Olive's, like an instructor explaining a particularly important fact. He smiled a glinting, hungry smile. "It's because of your *house,* Olive."

"My house," Olive echoed.

"The simple truth is, it should not be *your* house," Doctor Widdecombe said gently. The oil lamp flared, edging his huge body with ripples of darkness. "And it *isn't* your house. It requires—no, it *deserves* a great magician to inhabit it, to make use of its treasures, its legacy, its wealth of knowledge. It deserves a worthy heir. And you, Olive, as I have said from the start, are simply an ordinary little girl." Doctor Widdecombe placed one heavy hand on Olive's shoulder. "But now that you know so much, and remain so stubborn, we have no choice but to get rid of you permanently."

A flood of ice filled Olive's body. She shuddered as the truth sank in: They were stuck in a closet inside an enemy's house, blockaded by two powerful witches, with her parents sound asleep just a few feet away. They were trapped.

Rutherford's mind had clearly leaped to the same conclusion. "What about Walter?" he asked, stalling. "Did he fool me with his thoughts too? Or didn't he know anything about this?"

Doctor Widdecombe and Delora exchanged a bemused smile.

"Walter knows nothing at all," said Doctor Widdecombe.

"I have been burdened with him since my sister passed into the dark realm," said Delora. "She was as much a simpleton as Walter, but I promised to teach him all I could." Delora gave a lofty sigh. "However, there are some who just cannot be taught."

"Walter was merely supposed to keep an eye on you," Doctor Widdecombe added. "His task was to report back to us about your doings, nothing more."

Olive frowned. "If he wasn't working with you, then why did he try to sneak into my house? Who was he going to steal the McMartins' things for? Why—"

"That's enough," said Doctor Widdecombe, brushing her words away with a wave of his hand. "As much as I enjoy teaching the young, there comes a time for words to end and for actions to take their place. Hold still, Olive," he continued, tugging a silk handkerchief out of his pocket. His other hand tightened its grip on her shoulder. "This first part is completely painless."

He cupped the handkerchief in his palm. Olive jerked backward, but Doctor Widdecombe's hand on her shoulder was too heavy and too strong. She watched the handkerchief coming closer, about to cover her nose and mouth, and she caught the faintest whiff of something bitter rising from the fabric.

But before he could clamp the cloth over Olive's face, a change came over Doctor Widdecombe. The same change came over Delora, who was still hovering in the flickering hallway just behind him. Simultaneously, they stiffened, their faces going perfectly blank, as if they'd been listening to a long and detailed lecture on the merits of unwaxed dental floss. Their bodies rocked slowly backward. Then, like two mismatched dominoes, they toppled over, revealing Walter standing in the hallway behind them, his empty hands still raised in their direction.

Their bodies hit the floor with a resounding crash. The lamp that Delora had been clutching shattered on the floorboards, its oil spattering from the broken glass base, its flames shooting upward and outward into a roaring fountain of fire.

21

WALTER WAVERED AT the edge of the burning puddle, looking too stunned to move.

"We need to stifle the fire!" Rutherford shouted. "Hurry!"

Olive lunged back into the closet, grabbing a heavy wool coat from its hanger. She flew back through the door, tossing the outspread cloth over the flame, and Rutherford stomped on it with both slippered feet.

Almost as quickly as it had begun, the fire was out. Darkness filled the hallway once again, except for the beam of Rutherford's flashlight, which was now focused on Walter's face.

"Mmm...sorry..." said Walter, shifting awkwardly on his skinny legs. "I didn't think about the lamp."

"Are they dead?" Olive nudged the scorched coat

aside to look at Doctor Widdecombe and Delora. The fire had begun to singe Delora's flowing black skirts, but her face was still completely blank.

"Mmm . . . no. They're just frozen. I think."

"How did you do that?" Rutherford asked. He stared at Walter's empty hands. "You can perform spontaneous spell-casting?"

"I don't know," said Walter. "I didn't know I could."

"What's spontaneous spell-casting?" Olive turned to Rutherford.

"It's magic performed without the use of herbs or symbols or tools of any kind," Rutherford explained. From the way his flashlight beam began to bounce in the smoky air, Olive knew that he was jiggling very excitedly. "Only force of will, concentration of powers, and occasional words are required. It takes a *highly* gifted witch to do it."

Olive remembered Annabelle McMartin's hand flicking through the stormy air above the painted lake, lifting the spectacles from Olive's neck, tossing a ball of fire that exploded against Lucinda Nivens's chest. "I've seen Annabelle do it," she murmured.

"I'm not working for her. I swear," Walter rumbled. "I knew something was wrong. Two days ago, I found your parents in here. I thought—if I had a spellbook, I might find a way to get rid of the shades. Or I could stop Aunt Delora and Doctor Uncle—I mean Uncle Doctor—I mean—"

"But you were looking for the grimoire long before that," said Olive, a sliver of suspicion still prickling her mind. "And I saw you in the garden, looking for ingredients."

Walter's Adam's apple bobbed. "I wanted to make them proud. Before I knew." He looked down at the silent figures of his aunt and uncle. "And I guess I didn't need ingredients anyway."

"No," said Olive, gazing at Doctor Widdecome. His broad belly rose and fell peacefully. "I guess you didn't."

"Fascinating," Rutherford breathed.

"So, can you wiggle your fingers or something and wake my parents?" Olive asked.

Walter's eyes widened. "Mmm . . ." he rumbled. "I'm not sure. This was the first time it worked." He held up his hands, aiming them shakily at the back of the closet. "I'll try. But it might freeze them instead . . ."

"Never mind," said Rutherford quickly. "There's somebody else who'll know exactly what to do."

As it happened, Mrs. Dewey owned a rolling cart, which she kept on her patio to wheel potted plants in and out of the sun. This made moving four inert bodies from the Nivenses' house to the Deweys' considerably easier. However, it still took the collected efforts of Olive, Rutherford, Mrs. Dewey, and Walter to squish the heap that was Doctor Widdecombe onto the cart and out through the back door.

The hard work didn't bother Olive one bit. Relief and joy surrounded her like a warm, fuzzy blanket. She felt herself beginning to relax, to cuddle down into the comfort of it . . . and still, something kept tugging at the blanket's edge, uncovering her toes to the cold.

Once everyone was arranged in Mrs. Dewey's kitchen, the Dunwoodys propped comfortably in chairs, and Doctor Widdecombe and Delora plopped uncomfortably in a corner of the floor, Mrs. Dewey and Rutherford sprang into action, grinding tiny star-shaped seeds into powder, measuring cups of sugar and something equally pale and sparkly that *wasn't* sugar, and heating water in the big brass teapot. Olive stood between her parents, not wanting to take her hands off of their sleeping shoulders. A persistent, chilly wrongness prickled at the back of her neck.

"Well, I am absolutely *livid*," said Mrs. Dewey, pounding some small silvery pods with a meat-tenderizing hammer. "I know Byron and Delora can be arrogant at times, but I had no idea that they were so greedy, so short-sighted, and so *monstrous* as to do a thing like this. I am so sorry, Olive," she went on, with a *wham* that sent one pod flying toward Mr. Dunwoody's nose. It bounced off one nostril and landed in his lap. Mr. Dunwoody didn't move.

"I would never have brought them here if I had suspected . . ." Mrs. Dewey gave the pods another *wham*.

"If it wouldn't be setting a bad example for the three of you, I would be burying them in the garden manure right now."

"Mmm . . . What *are* you going to do with them?" Walter asked, from his spot beside the warm stove.

"We could put them Elsewhere," said Rutherford.

"*No,*" said Olive.

"I'll come up with something appropriate," said Mrs. Dewey, sweeping the crushed pods into a blue china bowl. "Walter, would you hand me that teapot, please?"

As Mrs. Dewey whisked the steaming water into the bowl, sprinkling the sparkly not-sugar over the top, Olive crouched down between her parents. Mr. Dunwoody let out a snore.

"What happens when they wake up?" she asked Mrs. Dewey. "What do we tell them? Will they remember everything?"

"That's what *these* are for," said Mrs. Dewey, reaching for one of the many cookie jars that stood on her kitchen shelves. She whipped off the lid. "My Dutch-cocoa-sour-cream swirls. Your parents will wake up disoriented and hungry, and these will erase their recent memories. The more they eat, the more will be erased. Don't worry, Olive," she went on, as Olive's eyes widened. "I'll make sure to stop them long before they forget the important things."

"If you could make them forget my last math grade, that would be fine," said Olive.

Mrs. Dewey smiled. "I'll see what I can do."

The blue bowl was beginning to send up wafts of curly green steam, which smelled like mint and early-summer mornings. Mrs. Dewey ladled the steaming liquid into two teacups and sprinkled a pinch of ground star seeds over the tops. "Now, stay back, you two, or you'll be up all night," she warned Olive and Rutherford. Then she held the cups under Mr. and Mrs. Dunwoody's softly snoring noses.

Olive watched the sea-green steam swirl up over her parents' faces. Her father's eyebrows twitched. Her mother's eyelashes fluttered. Together, they raised their heads and opened their eyes, which focused, at the very same instant, on Olive.

"Olive!" they both shouted, grasping her hands.

"You're all right!" said her mother, brushing the hair from Olive's face.

"They didn't take you too, did they? The masked intruders?" her father demanded.

"I *thought* they were too tall to be trick-or-treaters," said Mrs. Dunwoody.

"Yes, but as we discussed before we let them in, there are sufficient outliers to the rules of average height and weight to make it not impossible that they were children," said Mr. Dunwoody.

"Not impossible, but unlikely," said Mrs. Dunwoody. "Statistically speaking, I would guess that children under the age of fourteen—pre-high-school, that is—who weigh approximately three hundred pounds and are nearly six feet tall would make up a percentage of—"

"You must be hungry after that ordeal, Alec and Alice," said Mrs. Dewey, sweeping in with a plateful of cookies.

"You are absolutely right, Lydia," said Mr. Dunwoody, taking a large bite of a Dutch-cocoa-sour-cream swirl. "Thank you. Now, what was I saying?"

"I believe . . ." Mrs. Dunwoody hesitated, chewing. "These are delicious, Lydia. Thank you very much. I believe *I* was saying something."

"Would either of you care for a cup of tea? Or coffee?" Mrs. Dewey offered.

"Coffee," said Mr. and Mrs. Dunwoody simultaneously.

"Were we talking about Halloween?" Mrs. Dunwoody resumed.

"I could have sworn we were discussing prime numbers." Mr. Dunwoody rubbed his forehead. Then he paused, patting slowly at the space around both of his eyes. "I'm afraid I can't remember where I left my glasses."

"I'll find them," Olive promised, beaming at Mr. Dunwoody.

Mr. Dunwoody beamed blindly back up at her.

"I'll be right back!" she called from the kitchen doorway.

"What did Olive say she was going to do?" she heard her father ask as she bolted through the back door and flew across Mrs. Dewey's yard.

Outside, the sky was still dark, and the air was still cold. This night had seemed to go on forever, yet there wasn't even a streak of blue on the horizon. Frost clung to the lawns, coating each blade of grass with hazy silver.

Olive galloped around the hedge up the front porch steps, too overjoyed to notice that the lights in the entry and the library had gone out once again. She flipped the switch beside the front door, and the old stone house seemed to welcome her in, its golden light sweeping around her like protective arms.

Her father's glasses would be waiting safely on the table beside Olive's bed, just where she had left them. Olive jogged up the stairs. Her parents were safe, and they were coming home, and everything was—

Everything was—

Olive's steps slowed.

At the top of the stairs, everything was dark. This wasn't the darkness of a room without lights; it was solid darkness. Aggressive darkness. A wall of blackness waited for her, extending across the hall from

Olive's bedroom all the way to her parents' door—a living wall, rippling with hands and claws and teeth and faces.

Olive froze, balanced on the edge of two stairs.

There was the soft rustle of silk, and the wall parted, giving way to a pretty woman in a long white gown.

Annabelle McMartin, with her painted gold eyes and small, chilly smile stepped slowly toward the head of the staircase. Beside her strode a glossy black cat, sleek and silent as a panther. Behind them both, like a long black bridal train, the retinue of monstrous shadows rippled and shifted, spidery legs skittering, jaws gaping with sharpened teeth.

Olive knew what had been prickling at the back of her mind.

She had left the house unguarded for far too long.

"There you are, Olive Dunwoody," Annabelle said sweetly. "We wondered when you would be back."

She raised one hand, fingers sweeping daintily through the air.

The last of the lights went out.

S URROUNDED BY FREEZING darkness, Olive felt herself being dragged along the hallway, toward her parents' bedroom door. Damp fins and scaly limbs pushed her through, leaving their burning cold touch on her skin. The bedroom was dark, its windows glazed with night sky. Wheeling out of reach of the shades, Olive pressed her back to the wall between the two large paintings. She could feel her heartbeat against the plaster.

Annabelle's white gown moved like mist through the darkness. Leopold walked beside her, invisible but for his bright green eyes.

"I'm here to take back what was mine," said Annabelle in her sugary voice. "In fact, I've already begun. She brushed back a wave of long, dark hair, revealing the gold filigreed locket glittering softly against the strand of pearls. Annabelle touched the locket gently. "I had something new to put inside of it," she said. A smile curled on her face like a poisonous pink flower.

Olive felt a spiral of horror opening inside of her, pulling everything else to its depths. "I don't know what you're planning to do," she said, fighting to keep her voice steady, "but my friends will be here any minute."

"That's right! They will!" Annabelle clasped her hands together, as though Olive had said that a throng of party guests was about to arrive. "And they will come rushing up here to save you, and then something *delightful* will happen."

Her cold, painted hand touched Olive's arm, steering her toward the painting of the old sailing ship. "Put on the spectacles, Olive," she said, in a voice that wasn't sugary anymore.

Olive swallowed. Keeping the ribbon securely around her neck, she placed the spectacles on her nose.

"Now, look into the painting. Don't worry," Annabelle added lightly. "I'm not going to push you in."

And I'm not going to trust a word you say, thought Olive, bracing both legs against the wall. Slowly, with both hands locked around the picture frame, she pressed her face through the softening canvas.

A blast of salty wind tousled her hair. Far below her,

so far that if she plunged into them she would never reach the frame again, rolled the painted waves of the deep purple sea. In the middle distance, the sailing ship creaked, rocking slowly back and forth. Everything was just as it had been before—except now, in the center of that wooden ship's deck, there stood a tiny human figure. It was a girl, Olive could tell. A gangly girl with brownish hair. And a striped sweater. And a terrified expression on her tiny, painted face.

A wave of nausea roiled through Olive's body. Spotting Olive, the distant girl began to wave both arms, jumping desperately up and down. She might have been shouting something, but over the roar of the ocean, Olive could not hear it.

She jerked her head back through the frame.

"Is—is—" she choked, staring up into Annabelle's smiling face. "Is that supposed to be *me*?"

"A good likeness, isn't it?" Annabelle nodded admiringly at the painting. "Of course, Grandfather can't paint a *true* portrait without its subject present, and he had to add the figure in a hurry . . . but from a distance, it should fool even your own family. Don't you agree?"

Olive swallowed the sick sensation rising in her throat. "He's here?" she managed. "In the house?"

"Oh, he's far from here by now," said Annabelle. Her smile curved higher. "Hard at work. Safe and sound."

Stomach twisting, Olive stared back at that tiny, desperate figure on the deck of the ship. Why would Aldous strand a *fake* Olive there, when the *real* Olive—the one who was still in his way—remained free? And with this fake Olive in plain sight in her parents' bedroom, would anyone even wonder what had happened to the real Olive, before it was much too late . . . ?

"You're figuring out how it will work, aren't you, Olive?" Annabelle asked. "Your friends and family will search the house for you, and oh, how horrified they'll be to spot you trapped inside the painting! Fortunately, Leopold will be waiting for them. He'll explain how he's escaped my clutches, and expressing his concern for you, he'll hold the entrance open while all of your allies plop willingly inside." Annabelle gave a delighted little shrug. "And then we'll simply leave them there! Won't we, Leopold?"

The black cat kept silent.

"Won't we, Leopold?" Annabelle repeated, giving him a kick with her pointed white shoe.

"Don't!" Olive cried.

Leopold's eyes didn't leave the floor. "Yes, miss," he said softly, getting back to his feet.

"What about me?" Olive asked, drawing Annabelle's attention away from the cat. "What are you going to do?"

"Oh, you'll be nearby," said Annabelle. "Someplace where you can be *alone*. Because that's what you deserve, Olive." Annabelle bent until her painted gold eyes were level with Olive's. "For the damage you've done to my family, you deserve to be all alone, for a very, very long time. I believe I'll tie you to a tree deep in the painted forest. That's fitting, don't you think?" Annabelle's voice dropped to a honeyed murmur. "The very first bit of Elsewhere you invaded will also be your very last."

Olive stared hard into Annabelle's eyes. "I have a question," she managed.

Annabelle's head tilted graciously to one side. "Yes?"

Please, Olive thought. *I trust you. I trust you. I trust you.*

"How are you going to trap any of us Elsewhere, if you have no way to get inside?" Olive yanked the spectacles over her head so hard that the ribbon ripped several strands of her hair. She flung them toward the black cat. *"Run, Leopold!"*

There was an instant where Olive felt everything floating, as the spectacles sailed through the air, and the meaning of her words passed through Annabelle's and Leopold's minds. But Leopold caught on a split second faster. Before Annabelle could move, he'd caught the spectacles too. In a smooth, silent motion, he streaked from the bedroom, the spectacles clamped between his teeth.

Annabelle's face twisted, her rosebud mouth and long-lashed eyes turning wide and ugly with rage.

"Come back here, Leopold!" she shrieked. *"I will DESTROY you!"* She tore into the hallway after the cat, with the roaring shades and Olive rushing behind her.

Olive reached the head of the stairs just in time to watch Leopold hit the floor of the lower hall and zoom into the library. She didn't stop to wonder why, but inside the pitch-dark house, she could see Leopold perfectly, thanks to the warm, flickering light that poured through the library doors.

Annabelle chased him into the library, the shades swarming behind her. Olive jumped down the last several steps, stumbling and scrambling on all fours into the house's largest room. What she saw hit her like a wall of frigid water.

Leopold sat perfectly still, inches from the huge fire that crackled in the fireplace—close enough to the flames that Annabelle had to keep her distance. The living portrait had halted a few feet away, rocking back and forth in rage, while the fire glimmered over her painted skin. The shades had scattered backward, into the arc of shadows just beyond the firelight. Olive took in the shifting shades, the spectacles glinting in the cat's teeth, the furious portrait looming over him. But Leopold's eyes weren't fixed on Annabelle. They were fixed on something behind her. Something lurking in the shadows, just beyond one worn velvet chair.

Annabelle's voice was soft and dangerous. "What are you thinking, you stupid beast?" she murmured. The black cat didn't stir. "Do you think you can escape me in my own house?"

"It isn't your house," said a voice.

Annabelle's head shot up, her eyes narrowing. From behind the velvet chair, a blotch of darkness glided into the pool of firelight. It flickered into the figure of a very small, very old woman. The shade of Ms. McMartin approached the portrait of Annabelle with slow, ladylike steps.

Annabelle's little rosebud mouth opened very slightly, but no sound came out.

"You recognize me, don't you?" said Ms. McMartin, in Annabelle's own sugary voice. Her white hair darkened, and her wrinkled skin pulled smooth.

Annabelle took a tiny step backward.

"You know who I am," the shade murmured. "And yet you don't know me. But I know *you*."

"What is this?" Annabelle whispered, her voice the hiss of a cornered snake. "What do you think you know?"

"I know what we are," Ms. McMartin said gently. Her smoky hair paled to white again. "What we have become."

Olive darted into the room, dropping to her knees next to Leopold. Ms. McMartin's eyes followed her.

"Would you make this child an orphan?" she asked Annabelle. "Would you do to her what was done to you?"

Annabelle's lips tightened. "Grandfather did what he had to do to protect this house and this family."

"Was it worth protecting?" Ms. McMartin asked. Outside the ring of firelight, the shadows thrashed and muttered. Eely fingers and tooth-filled jaws snapped against the glow. Ms. McMartin seemed not to notice. "I think not," she answered herself. "And in time, you would have come to think so too."

The shades stretched and roared against the boundary of the light.

Annabelle's face tensed, like a wire strung up to slice someone's throat. "You are wrong," she snarled. "I am proud to belong to this family. You *lie*."

"Would you like to see?" Ms. McMartin asked, very softly. "Would you like to see what serving this family has done to us? What a lifetime of selfishness and loneliness and regret brings?" Her voice dropped even lower, as delicate and dusty as a moth's wing. "Would you like to see what has become of us by the end?" she breathed. "To see yourself as you truly are?"

Ms. McMartin glided away from the circle of firelight. The rest of the shades recoiled, leaving her alone as she crossed the worn carpet. She turned back, facing the fire, and Olive could see the last traces of her misty features disappearing, sinking into the black silhouette that had been hidden underneath all along.

The soft, upswept hair vanished from her head. The pearls and blouse and skirt disappeared. Her face seemed to melt, leaving empty eyes and a slit of mouth on a head like a misshapen black egg. Beneath its weight, her neck grew long and bent. Her shoulders rose, bony and hunched, and her legs bent into a permanent, animal crouch. Rope-thin arms stretched beyond her feet and across the floor, fingers groping blindly, like long, black worms.

What was left wasn't Ms. McMartin, or even an outline of Ms. McMartin. What was left was an inhuman, broken, withered thing. It was a thing so hideous that instead of fearing it, Olive felt nothing but pity.

This was the real Annabelle McMartin. Orphaned. Twisted. Deserted. Unloved.

Olive didn't realize that she had been inching forward until she felt Annabelle's cold hand brush against her side. She glanced up. The portrait stood beside her, eyes wide with horror.

"Will you trust me, Olive?" the thing that had been Ms. McMartin whispered through the darkness.

Olive swallowed. All the times when she had trusted the wrong people—Mrs. Nivens, Doctor

Widdecombe and Delora, Annabelle herself—sent regret and pain and fear throbbing through her, like fingers pressing on a bruise. She looked at the withered silhouette.

"I'll trust you," she whispered back.

The black form lumbered out of the shadows, dragging itself across the carpet. Olive felt its terrible cold crash into her, sinking through her skin and muscle and bone. All that remained of Ms. McMartin—anger, loathing, loneliness, shame—sank inside of Olive as well. The mixture was so painful, she could barely move. For a split second, Olive was sure she had been tricked again, that this monster would hold her until she froze to death. But then she heard Ms. McMartin's soft voice.

"Do as I do," the shade whispered. Its words seemed to come from inside Olive's own mind, where no one else could hear. "Follow me." The shade threw its long, shriveled arms around the portrait of Annabelle. With a burst of effort, Olive did the same, keeping her arms inside the shadowy limbs. She felt the writhing coldness of Annabelle's body against the deeper, numbing chill of her own, which was closed inside the shade like a leaf in ice. The shade's enveloping presence seemed to cut off everything else: the hissing of the other shades, Annabelle's furious screams, the pounding of her own heartbeat.

"Into the fire," the shade breathed.

Annabelle staggered backward, trying to break free, but Olive held on tight. Locked together, Olive, the shade of Ms. McMartin, and the portrait of Annabelle plunged over the hearth, into the massive fireplace.

The flames took Annabelle instantly. The oil paint of her body turned into a streak of fire before she had time to speak. Olive squeezed her eyes shut, feeling the chill of the shade surrounding her while the burst of the conflagration warmed her face, and while Annabelle let out a scream that echoed away up the chimney on a burst of thick black smoke.

When Olive opened her eyes at last, she could see that her shivering arms held nothing at all.

Annabelle's locket glimmered in the flames at her feet. There was a brief moment when Olive thought, *I'm standing in a fire, and I can't even feel it!*—and then a soft, tickling warmth began to rise from her feet toward her ankles. Olive felt the chill of Ms. McMartin's presence slipping away, falling upward, as though gravity had turned upside down. A figure made of mist, delicate as an exhalation, rose up the chimney with the trails of smoke. Olive saw soft white hair and a string of pearls dissolving, untangling into wisps, floating into the tiny square of violet sky high above.

The fire that licked at Olive's legs was suddenly hot and threatening. She stumbled out of the fire-place just as the cuffs of her jeans began to scorch. "Leopold," she began, falling on her knees beside the cat. "Are you—"

The rest of her words were buried in the incoming roar of the McMartin shades.

OLIVE AND LEOPOLD crouched together on the library floor. The room had taken on a strange, sickly haze, like the sky before a storm, and Olive could barely keep her eyes open against the force of the rising wind.

The shades had collected into a streak of motion. Their barreling black mass tore around the room, twisting into a cyclone of claws and tentacles and sharp teeth. The heavy velvet curtains whipped and snapped as they roared past. Books tumbled from the shelves, their pages flapping as they blew across the carpets. Papers scattered from the Dunwoodys' desks like snowflakes in a blizzard. The chandelier swung wildly on its chain.

Olive felt a surge of cold as the black wind moved

over her, *through* her, stealing the air straight out of her lungs. Her throat burned. Then the wind twisted away once more, and the walls themselves seemed to darken, as if they'd been coated with black frost, or a layer of ash.

Leopold's sleek fur rubbed against her arm. "Are you all right, miss?" he shouted, pinning the spectacles to the rug with one paw.

"I'm fine," Olive gasped. "I'm—"

A fresh gust of cold crashed over her. A thousand needles of ice pricked her skin, sliding through her with their stinging, invisible threads.

The roar filling the room grew worse.

"Shall I summon help?" Leopold shouted.

A blast of freezing air threw the cat aside. Olive heard his claws tearing at the rug as the black wind shoved him, hissing and thrashing, into the hall. The library doors slammed shut behind him.

They are part of this house, Horatio's voice whispered in Olive's memory. *And we belong to this house . . .*

Olive covered her head as the shades rushed inward again, and the heavy brass chandelier came plummeting down, smashing into Mr. Dunwoody's desk. Shards of broken glass cascaded through the dim air.

The room was growing darker still. Behind Olive, the fire had died to a few guttering embers, which were jerked and dulled by each shift of the wind. Olive crept backward, huddling against the hearth. Her hands and feet seemed to have disappeared. Only a soft tingling sensation in her wrists and ankles told her where they should have been.

She felt so heavy. And so, so cold.

She had only felt this cold once in her life: in the attic of the old stone house, facing the shadowy creature that was all that was left of Aldous McMartin. Then, as now, she had felt her body begin to give up without asking her brain's permission. Exhaustion had taken over. She'd almost stopped fighting . . . and then . . .

Like a red-hearted coal bursting back into flames, an idea opened in Olive's mind.

Wobbling to her feet, Olive lurched toward the center of the room. The rippling curtains and whirling shades eclipsed the faint light coming through the windows, and the wind was strong enough to nearly knock her backward. Bits of glass and paper sliced through the air. A heavy porcelain vase flew past her, shattering against the wall. Fallen books tumbled around her feet.

Olive knelt down, groping blindly over the rug until she'd amassed a heap of books and papers. She hoped that they were the very dullest books in the room—novels about Victorian dowagers sipping tea, or encyclopedias of socks perhaps—but there wasn't time to check. Crawling, shoving the pile ahead of her, she inched back across the room toward the fireplace. The wind tore at her hair, ripping the breath out of her body.

The fire had died to a faint red glow in the distance. Olive struggled forward, moving closer, closer, almost there—

—until a solid weight of cold plunged suddenly around her.

The library went completely still.

In the icy hush that followed, Olive realized that the shades had enclosed her. They were layered one on top of the other—one *inside* the other—trapping Olive at their core. It was like being inside the shade of Ms. McMartin, only fifty times colder and heavier. Instead of being coated with ice, she was crushed by a frozen avalanche.

At the center of the frigid darkness, Olive felt her racing heart begin to slow. Frost prickled on her eyelashes and inside her nose. Each breath stung. Her bones shook in their sockets. Cold could kill you, Olive knew, almost like a poison. It would shut her body down, bit by bit. Worse still, she could feel the shades' hatred—their hatred of *her*—seeping through her entire body. Their voices hissed inside her brain.

Liar. Trespasser. Our house.

She blinked, frost stinging in her eyes. Before her,

the fire seemed to waver and split into several pieces, which went floating off around the room. Olive tried to keep her eyes on the real fire glimmering in the dimness. She remembered Morton's Halloween costume, flickering through the crowded gym, guiding her closer. She remembered the glint of Leopold's eyes in the darkness of the basement.

They had trusted her.

She wouldn't let them be wrong.

With numb hands, she gave the pile of books anther shove forward. She had to reach that fire.

Liar. Our house.

The hiss swelled to a roar inside her brain. Coldness thickened around her heart, the hatred of the entire McMartin clan pinning her to the floor.

Olive wormed forward, and felt the rug beneath her shift to tile. She'd reached the hearth. *Come on,* she told herself. *Don't give in.*

On trembling arms, she pulled herself into the warm ashes of the grate. The shades came with her, a black, thrashing, whispering armor. One ember still burned beneath the ash. Shaking so hard that she nearly lost her grip, Olive grabbed the nearest book and held its pages to the glow.

The ember gave a small red flare, and then, very slowly, it winked out.

Olive could hear the McMartins' laughter inside of

her own head. It was the only sound in that huge room. There was only the dark and the cold, and that awful sound—and the slam of two heavy wooden doors.

A burst of gentle warmth, like water gushing into a bathtub, flowed around Olive's body. She could hear the books she'd dragged along crackling into flames, and the sound of hissing laughter turning to shrieks. But these were too faint and far off for Olive to care. She smiled, rolling over in the warmth, as a flower of golden light filled the massive fireplace.

Olive felt a weight lifting away, layer by layer. Wisps of mist rose up the chimney, carrying empty-eyed faces, fading hands. She blinked up the long, dark column at the shades dissolving softly into the night air beyond.

The fire sank into ashes as suddenly as it had begun. The scorched books and papers surrounding her seemed to vanish. Olive lay for a minute, breathing the warm, wonderful air, realizing that she was still awake and alive. Then, cautiously, she inched out of the fireplace to find Walter, Rutherford, Morton, and all three cats staring down at her.

"Oh, Olive," sighed Horatio, his eyes flickering over Olive's sooty clothes. "You are absolutely *filthy*."

24

IN MS. TEEDLEBAUM'S art class, Olive had seen a film about art restorers at work on the ceiling of an old church in Italy. The ceiling was covered by a very old, very famous painting. Centuries of dust and smoke and dirt and dampness had covered the painting so gradually that no one had even noticed the change. But when the art restorers were done, the ancient painting looked new again. Its reds were *red*. Its blues were *blue*. What had been beautiful in spite of its darkness was suddenly, almost blindingly bright.

This was what the old stone house looked like as Olive and her friends gazed around.

Picture frames gleamed like buttery gold on the papered walls. Chandeliers sparkled from the ceilings. Stained glass gleamed and glittered in the windowpanes. In the library, each fallen book and toppled chair and broken lightbulb had returned to its place, better than new.

Everyone halted in the front entryway like a swarm of bugs smacking into a windshield. They stared up at the colorful walls and the high ceilings and the gleaming floors, where slips of dawn light were just beginning to glimmer.

"Wow," Walter breathed.

"Fascinating," whispered Rutherford.

Olive put out one hand, running her palm along the old stone wall. Instead of the familiar chill, she felt only a faint warmth, like the skin of something asleep, but alive.

"I love it," she said softly.

Inside her own bedroom, Olive shut the curtains to keep Morton safe from the rising sun. Walter arranged his long, bony body on Olive's much-too-small vanity chair. Morton sat on the floor, far from the reach of the bedside lamp, and Rutherford stood near the door. Olive and the three cats occupied the bed, Horatio seated grandly at its foot, Leopold keeping close to Olive, and Harvey pouncing at imaginary enemies in the rumples of Olive's bedspread.

"Walter," Olive began, turning toward the vanity, "it was *you* who made that fire?"

"Mmm—I just *lit* it," said Walter. "Rutherford's the one who knew what you were trying to do."

"Spontaneous spell-casting," said Rutherford admiringly. "I saw it for myself this time."

Olive smiled at Rutherford. "Thank you," she said. "All of you."

"Thank *you*, miss," said Leopold. "It's due to you that Annabelle McMartin is gone for good."

Olive hugged her knees to her chest. She patted the spectacles that were tucked safely back inside her collar. "She's gone," she said softly. "She's *really* gone. And I know I should be glad, but—but I didn't get her to tell me where Morton's parents are." Olive looked down at the floor, but she couldn't meet Morton's eyes. "I'm so sorry, Morton."

Morton didn't answer.

Harvey attacked a rumple in the bedspread, smashing it flat. "There," he announced in a faint British accent. "I perceived that this room was bugged." He turned to Leopold. "Now that the last of those bugs has been squashed, we can proceed with Agent 411's debriefing."

Leopold stiffened. "I was not able to gather much information, I'm afraid," he began, in a voice that was even gruffer than usual. "Annabelle kept me locked in a small box. I was not able to see where we went or how we got there. If I had to guess, I would say that we were underground—a situation with which I am quite familiar."

"And then," Horatio prompted, "you helped her release Aldous from his portrait?"

Head bowed, Leopold looked down at the bed-spread. "I resisted for as long as possible," he said softly. Everyone fell silent. The truth that Olive and Leopold had already known—that Aldous McMartin was free—filled the room like a freezing wind.

"Don't worry, Leopold," Olive said at last. "It's my fault that you had to go with Annabelle in the first place. The only thing that really matters is that you're safe, and you're back home with us." She stroked Leopold's head gently. It grew a tiny bit less bowed.

"As for our more unexpected enemies," said Rutherford, changing the subject, "my grandmother's plan for Delora and Doctor Widdecombe involves a huge bag of Dutch-cocoa-sour-cream swirls and two one-way tickets to Transylvania. So Walter is free of his highly unfulfilling apprenticeship."

"And I'm going to stay here," Walter said, smiling shyly. He rearranged his legs over the vanity chair, looking like a giraffe in a kindergarten classroom. "Next door. Mrs. Dewey is going to make me *her* apprentice." His eyes traveled to Olive. "So I can help you. If—mmm—if you'd like."

Morton hopped suddenly to his feet.

"I didn't say you could stay in my house," he said, marching up to Walter with his arms tightly folded. His head didn't reach the seated Walter's chin. "You'll keep changing things and moving things. And you didn't even *ask*."

Walter blinked. "I'm sorry," he said. "You're right. We should have asked you first."

"Yes," said Morton. "You should have."

"So . . . mmm . . ."

"I give you permission to stay in my house," said Morton grandly. He cast a glance back at Olive. "And I'm going to stay there too."

"What?" Olive sucked in a breath. "Morton, don't you remember how dangerous it could be, if—"

"Lucinda lived outside for years and years, in that very same house," Morton interrupted her. "Nobody even noticed there was something wrong with her. And I'm *much* smarter than she was. Besides, I'm only going to stay there until we find my parents. I know what you're going to say," he went on, before Olive could argue. He put on a high, squeaky voice. *"But Morton, that could take a long, long time!"*

"I don't sound like that!" Olive objected.

"But it won't take a long time," Morton plowed on. "Because I'm going to find them. And Walter will be my bodyguard. Right?"

"Mmm . . . Right," said Walter, looking slightly stunned. "Yes."

"I'll even let you keep the spectacles," said Morton, chin in the air. "As long as you help me later. *If* I ask you to."

"Morton . . ." Olive let out a heavy breath. "I really tried," she whispered.

"I know." Morton stepped toward the end of the bed. "But I want to look for my parents *myself*. Just like you did."

Olive stared into Morton's round, determined face, and the truth settled over her like light slipping through a window. You could confine someone for two different reasons: Because you wanted to punish them, or because you wanted to keep them safe. But to the someone being confined, there really wasn't much difference. She turned toward the window, where the curtains were just beginning to brighten with the morning light.

"Then you had better get moving," she said. "It's almost sunrise."

From the front porch of the old stone house, Olive and the cats watched Morton and Walter walk away down the street. Morton was dressed in an old coat from the back of the Dunwoodys' closet, with a wide-brimmed hat planted securely over his tufty hair. The coat was too long for him. Each time Morton tripped, Walter waited patiently, watching over him like a long-legged crane guarding a fuzzy hatchling, until Morton had kicked the coat free.

The sun had just inched over the horizon. Its misty rays touched the rooftops of Linden Street, turning the brown lawns to silver. It spread across the houses, making windows sparkle and walls glow. Walter and

Morton disappeared through the front door of the tall gray house just as the sunbeams washed over its weedy front lawn. Olive watched the door close behind them.

In the house beyond that, another door swung open. Olive smiled at the sight of her parents emerging onto Mrs. Dewey's stoop, blinking and squinting into the morning sunlight. Mrs. Dewey walked beside her mother, and Rutherford bounced and jiggled beside her father, leading them up the hill toward the old stone house.

"I'd better get my dad his glasses," said Olive, stepping back inside.

The moment she and the cats were through the door, Olive remembered something else—another precious object someone had left behind.

She hurried into the library, with the three cats beside her.

Still glimmering in the fireplace was Annabelle McMartin's locket. Its chain was tangled in the grate, and its filigreed gold was smudged with oily soot. Olive bent down and picked up the locket, feeling its familiar shape against the palm of her hand. Annabelle had said she had something *new* to put inside of it. Olive slipped one fingernail along the locket's edge, hearing the tiny click of its catch.

Inside the once-empty locket was a portrait. It was very small, made up of nothing but delicate lines of black ink, but it was perfectly clear whose portrait it was—and who had created it. Olive would have known that sharp brow, those hollow cheeks, and those sunken firepit eyes anywhere on earth, whether they were staring at her from an old photograph, or inside an antique locket, or from the just-finished portrait that had vanished from the attic of the old stone house.

"Well," said Horatio, from the rug beside her feet. "We know the best and worst of it all."

"What are you going to do now, miss?" Leopold asked.

Olive let out a long, heavy breath. "I think . . . I think I'm going to give my dad his glasses. And then I'm going to go to sleep for about three days."

Leopold nodded. "An excellent plan."

The cats glided ahead of her through the library doors. Olive watched Harvey bound for the staircase, muttering "Agent 1-800 returning to headquarters. Over and under. In and out." Leopold slipped toward the basement like a sleek black shadow.

Horatio paused in the doorway. "Sweet dreams, Olive," he said softly, over his shoulder. "And don't worry. We'll be standing guard."

About the author

JACQUELINE WEST is obsessed with stories where magic intersects with everyday life—from talking cats, to enchanted eyewear, to paintings as portals to other worlds. An award-winning poet, former teacher, and occasional musician, Jacqueline now lives with her husband in Red Wing, Minnesota. There she dreams of dusty libraries, secret passageways, and more adventures for Olive, Morton, and Rutherford.

Discover the other Books of Elsewhere:

VOLUME ONE

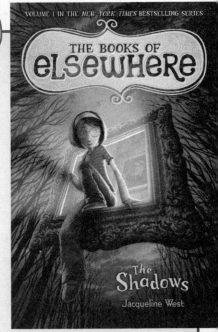

VOLUME 1 IN THE *NEW YORK TIMES* BESTSELLING SERIES

THE BOOKS OF ELSEWHERE

The Shadows

Jacqueline West

When eleven-year-old Olive moves into the crumbling old mansion on Linden Street, she's right to think there's something weird about the place—the creepy antique paintings, the three very unusual cats. But the weirdest thing? When Olive finds a pair of old-fashioned glasses in a drawer, she discovers she can travel *inside* the paintings to Elsewhere, a sinister world with strange secrets to keep. There she meets Morton, a small boy with a big temper. As he and Olive form an uneasy alliance, Olive finds herself caught in a plan darker and more dangerous than she could have imagined, confronting a power that wants to be rid of her by any means necessary. It's up to her to save the house from the shadows, before the lights go out for good.

VOLUME TWO

Olive is getting worried. With no way into the McMartins' enchanted paintings, her friend Morton is still trapped on the other side—in Elsewhere. Worse? The house's three guardian cats are absolutely no help at all (they're hiding something; Olive is sure of it). So when the new oddball kid next door mentions a grimoire—a *spellbook*—Olive feels

a breathless tug of excitement. If she can find the McMartins' spellbook, maybe she can help Morton escape Elsewhere for good. Unless, that is, the *book* finds *Olive* first.

VOLUME THREE

Some terrifying things have happened to Olive in the old stone house, but none as scary as starting . . . *junior high*. When she plummets through a hole in her backyard, however, Olive discovers two things that may change her mind: First, the wicked Annabelle McMartin is back. Second, there's a secret belowground that unlocks not one but *two* of Elsewhere's biggest, most powerful, most dangerous forces yet. With the house's guardian cats acting weird, her best friend hiding something huge, and her ally Morton starting to rebel, Olive isn't sure where to turn. Will she figure it out in time? Or will she be lured into Elsewhere and trapped there forever?